Each of Reba's movements seemed to mirror John's.

When she slowly reached up to lay her hand on the back of his collar, she felt his arm circle her waist. As she stretched up, he bent his head. Lost in his gaze and the exquisite anticipation of the moments that seemed inevitable now, she brushed a kiss against his cheek.

The increasing pressure of his hand on her back allowed her to move closer. She spread her fingers across the back of his head, and suddenly he was kissing her. The passion that they'd both denied, because it was inconvenient in their lives, spilled over suddenly…

Passion, rage and vulnerability. Arousal escalated out of control until it seemed that they were passing a point of no return. John held her close, his fingers exploring the sensitive skin behind her ear and moving to tangle in her hair.

Then suddenly he moved back. Holding her, his fingers tender against the skin of her cheek.

"Not here…"

"Not ever?" Reba felt her lower lip quiver at the thought.

"I didn't say that…"

Dear Reader,

Have you ever come across this? Two people whose eyes meet across a crowded room, they're inexorably drawn together and…they argue. I have and I'm happy to say that my two friends finally found their way through to making a relationship that wasn't based on conflict!

John and Reba are the same—they find themselves working together, and as soon as they set eyes on each other, they're drawn together. But they can't admit to being attracted to one another and so their suppressed passion takes the form of arguments. And when they decide that they must put their relationship on a more even keel, that presents them with a different challenge. How are they going to deal with the passion between them and find some outlet for it?

Thank you for reading Reba and John's story! I hope you enjoy it!

Annie x

CHILDREN'S DOC
TO HEAL HER HEART

———

ANNIE CLAYDON

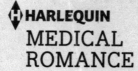

HARLEQUIN
MEDICAL
ROMANCE

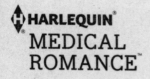

HARLEQUIN®
MEDICAL ROMANCE™

Recycling programs
for this product may
not exist in your area.

ISBN-13: 978-1-335-73782-3

Children's Doc to Heal Her Heart

Copyright © 2023 by Annie Claydon

For questions and comments about the quality of this book,
please contact us at CustomerService@Harlequin.com.

Harlequin Enterprises ULC
22 Adelaide St. West, 41st Floor
Toronto, Ontario M5H 4E3, Canada
www.Harlequin.com

Printed in U.S.A.

Cursed with a poor sense of direction and a propensity to read, **Annie Claydon** spent much of her childhood lost in books. A degree in English literature followed by a career in computing didn't lead directly to her perfect job—writing romance for Harlequin—but she has no regrets in taking the scenic route. She lives in London: a city where getting lost can be a joy.

Books by Annie Claydon

Harlequin Medical Romance

Dolphin Cove Vets

Healing the Vet's Heart

A Rival to Steal Her Heart
The Best Man and the Bridesmaid
Greek Island Fling to Forever
Falling for the Brooding Doc
The Doctor's Reunion to Remember
Risking It All for a Second Chance
From the Night Shift to Forever
Stranded with the Island Doctor
Snowbound by Her Off-Limits GP
Cinderella in the Surgeon's Castle

Visit the Author Profile page
at Harlequin.com for more titles.

CHAPTER ONE

REBA RUSHES IN where angels fear to tread... Rebekah Sloane's friends made the joke on a relatively regular basis, and usually she laughed and agreed with them. But right now she wasn't laughing.

She had rushed in, wanting this job because she knew that it would be challenging. When the position of music therapist in the paediatric department of the London and Surrey hospital had become vacant, it had been decided to expand the role from one day a week to two. Reba had sent off her CV, along with a hastily prepared document outlining some ideas for how she might make use of the extra time. She'd been interviewed by the head of rehabilitation services at the hospital and offered the post almost immediately, which Reba reckoned was not so much an indication that her skills were so much better than any other music therapist, but that there were precious few applicants who were willing to put their heads into a lion's mouth for a living.

But if she didn't take on the most difficult jobs, and her interview had left her in no doubt that this *would* be difficult, then how would she ever know what she was capable of doing? Her father had drummed that piece of wisdom into Reba from a very early age, although medicine wasn't quite what he'd had in mind as a career for his only child.

Working with children was always challenging, and that was one of the reasons why Reba loved it so much. Filling the shoes of the previous music therapist, who'd been highly respected and attached to the ward for the last twenty years, made things even harder. The tragic circumstances in which her predecessor had died meant that Reba was going to have to be sensitive and respectful in what she did. She'd been fully prepared for that, by the hospital's grassroots network and her new boss when he'd called her in for a chat before he'd put the final paperwork through the system.

But nobody—not one single person—had thought to prepare her for Dr John Thornton. He rose from his seat, grabbing a pile of papers from the chair opposite his desk so that she could sit down, and suddenly all that Reba could think of was that she'd omitted a very important entry on her list of challenges and solutions.

She could accept gorgeous and move on. Work had taught her how to face challenges, think outside the box and find ways forward. Life hadn't prepared her for someone who made all of the hairs stand up on the back of her neck and her fingers tingle.

He introduced himself, mentioning almost in passing that he was head of department here. And then he retreated behind his desk, taking his heady scent, his spectacular body and that gorgeous kissable mouth with him. Beyond reach. That was actually something of a relief.

'I'm sorry we haven't had a chance to meet up before now. Welcome to the department.'

'Thank you.' Reba smiled, and then decided she was probably smiling too much and straightened her face. 'I'm really looking forward to being here.'

'And that'll be Tuesdays and Fridays.'

'Yes, that's right. I work with private patients for the rest of the time. I gather that your previous music therapist was here for one day a week.'

'Yes, we've only recently received funding to increase that to two. We're all looking forward to working with you in expanding the role of music therapy in the department.'

Yeah. He was saying all of the right things but there wasn't any sincerity in his tone. He looked down at the copy of her CV that he'd plucked from one of the piles of files and papers on his desk, suddenly freeing Reba of the dilemma of deciding whether his eyes were grey or blue. Whatever colour, they were entrancing, and she'd noticed the dark rings beneath them as well. She'd bet they'd taken more than one sleepless night to form.

'Rebekah Sloane. No relation to Hans Sloane, the pianist?'

Good. A much-asked question that had a very simple answer, as long as no one thought too deeply about the realities of the situation. Most people worked that out from the blurb about her education, which skimmed as tactfully as possible over her chaotic childhood, travelling between the world's greatest cities, immersed in the all-encompassing belief that music was the key to almost everything.

'Actually, he's my father.'

He was still scanning the paper in front of him. 'And you play the piano yourself, I see.'

'Yes, I do, but when I'm working I find that sitting behind a keyboard sometimes separates me a little from the people I'm playing for. The violin's my first love, and it's much more portable as well.'

'This isn't a second interview but… I'm just interested…' He seemed to want permission to ask questions. That was fine with Reba, she had any number of answers.

'Yes?' She smiled encouragingly.

'What you do seems very different from a concert hall, where you're shushed if you don't keep quiet. You're looking for reactions.'

That was generally one of her answers. Dr John Thornton was perceptive, and she should concentrate on what he said, rather than letting those beautiful lips claim her attention.

'That's right. It's one of the reasons why I love playing sea shanties and folk songs, along with popular songs, because it's really hard not to join in and tap your feet. Although I know a little boy who loves Bach and has a whole robotic dance routine worked out to the *Ode to Joy*.'

That made him smile. 'That's not what music therapy is really about though, is it? Entertaining.'

'No, but it's my way in. Music reaches people, and who better to reach than a seven-year-old in hospital?' Hans would disagree with her there. Maybe if she'd grown up calling him *Daddy* then there would be some distinction between the father and the pianist, but Hans had always seemed like a much-loved mentor. She'd worked with what she had, trying to ignore the hurt over his obvious disappointment at her career choice.

It wasn't like Reba to allow her mind to wander during a business meeting, and she swallowed down the temptation to meet his gaze and tell him everything about herself. 'Isn't a connection what every medical professional seeks to establish? It doesn't really matter how someone does it, just that they do.'

There was something about the wry smile he gave in reply, which emphasised the gaunt lines on his face, and told Reba that John Thornton had been reaching out a little too much recently. That he was exhausted and too hurt to maintain his engagement with the people around him. She wondered if anyone had suggested he take a break and find a quiet place to let the sounds of the world flow past him, instead of blowing through him like a hurricane.

'Yes, you're right. Cathy had a very different way of working but…that's not really relevant, is it? No one wants to be told how their predecessor did things differently on their first day in a job.'

That she had an answer for. 'I still have plenty to learn. When I find that I can't take anything from the way that other people do things then I'll reckon I need to give this job up. And I'm very conscious of the need for continuity.'

He smiled suddenly. The first real smile she'd seen from him.

'Cathy may have used slightly different techniques from the ones you're outlining, but her approach was essentially the same as yours. She used who she was to connect with her patients.'

He was fiddling with one of the pens on his desk, and there was more he wanted to say. Reba waited. One of the things that Hans had taught her was that it was best to get your emotions off your chest. It was a good principle, although Hans' habit of shouting at the top of his voice wasn't always the best way to do it.

'I'm sure you already know what happened with Cathy...'

Reba didn't nod. Everyone had their own story to tell about any given situation, and it was clear that John was no exception to that.

'She'd been here for many years, and was very well liked. Cathy had a massive cardiac event in the staff break room here and even though there were doctors on hand, myself included, we couldn't save her. It's been difficult for everyone here.'

'I can only imagine.'

'But that's something *we* need to deal with, and we're doing so. The recent amendment in structure means that I'm not your line manager and you report direct to the head of rehabilitation, but the staff on the ward here are my responsibility. I'd like to work with you to make sure everything goes smoothly.'

It was nice of him to address the elephant in the room and just come out and say what everyone had gone around the houses in an effort to say tactfully. It would make broaching the subject much easier if she ever needed to. But still his gaunt face and embattled air was ringing alarm bells at the back of Reba's mind.

'I'm sure there'll be no problems...' She'd fallen into the habit of papering over the cracks and that wasn't true. Reba had been told outright that there might be problems, and she'd prepared herself for that. The flash of his grey-blue eyes told her that he wasn't buying it either.

Reba shrugged. 'Actually, I'm sure there may be one or two. But I'm determined to make this work, for me and for you. I think one of the ways I can do that is to accept that everyone would rather not be in the situation of needing a new music therapist, and not take that too personally. Maybe let them get to know me a bit and go from there.'

'Sounds like a constructive start.' His guarded smile crashed against her defences. 'I may be able to contribute something to that. Joanne's our trainee administrator, and when she steps fully into the job she'll be the one to greet new staff and take them on a tour. I asked her to write something up for me as an exercise and she's made a good job of it...'

He was obviously waiting for her reaction, and it occurred to Reba that this might be her first test. 'I'm used to being shown the way to the therapy room and left to get on with things. If Joanne would give me her tour I'd really appreciate it.'

Right answer. John nodded, reaching for the phone and then pausing. 'If you have any clinical questions, or want to know how things are supposed to work, then my door's always open. If you want to know how things *actually* work then Joanne's probably the one to ask.'

'Thanks, that'll save me some time. It usually takes me at least a couple of days to find the person in any department who knows how everything works.'

He nodded. 'Is there anything else you'd like to raise with me, Rebekah?'

'Nothing else. Apart from saying that most people call me Reba.' Rebekah always sounded as if she was in trouble about something, because generally when Hans called her that she was.

He nodded, picking up the phone and dialling an extension number. 'Joanne, Rebekah's here and I'm wondering whether you'll be able to give her the grand tour...'

What's in a name? It was probably just a slip of the tongue, but there was something in the way that John had called her Rebekah that said he was being careful to keep his distance. Maybe he was putting an emphasis on the idea that he wasn't her line manager, by maintaining a degree of formality. Or maybe something behind those beautiful, haunted eyes was telling her that she shouldn't get too close. He'd delivered the perfect welcome chat, and Reba was suddenly conscious that it had been all about how she felt, and he had never once betrayed his own feelings.

Rebekah. It was a lovely name, the old-fashioned spelling making it delightfully hers. But he should remember to call her Reba in future, since that was her preference. John swung his office chair back and forth, staring out of the window. Anyone who passed her in the street might say that she was beautiful, but that wouldn't be doing her justice. She was striking, with bright blue eyes and hair that was almost black, tied up at the back of her head in a slightly spiky arrangement that seemed to defy the laws of gravity. Her jaw was a little too broad and decisive and her gaze a little too frank for conventional beauty, but the effect was electrifying. And the way she moved had a rhythm about it all of its own, as if Reba was dancing to a melody that ordinary mortals weren't able to hear.

Reba. As he mouthed the name silently it almost felt like a kiss. That was going to be the biggest difficulty of all, because John had no time for this. He had a child to look after and a job to do, and both of them required every last drop of his emotional energy.

He had no spare capacity for grief either. Cathy had been a good friend, the mother of two grown-up daughters who'd applied a great deal of common sense to the situation when his sister had died and John had found that being the sole guardian of a four-year-old was a great deal more complicated than being a favourite uncle. Rosalie was five now, and beginning to settle after the upheaval of losing her mother, which was in no small part the result of Cathy's good advice and the good humour with which it had been given.

'You reckon pink?' He could practically see her now, standing in the sunny room that he was decorating as a bedroom for Rosalie. 'You're sure about that, John?'

He'd shrugged. 'Little girls like pink, don't they?'

Cathy had rolled her eyes. 'Sure they do. And they're made of sugar and spice as well…'

'All right. So what colour do you think, then?'

'You could always ask her. Only don't just give her a paint chart and tell her to pick something out. If she's anything like my eldest she'll decide she likes crimson and it'll give her nightmares.' Cathy had smirked at him. 'I made all these mistakes, so you don't have to.'

'How did you do it, then? When you were deciding what colour to paint the crimson over with?'

'Choose a few different colours that you think might be suitable. Then get some tester pots and paint squares on the wall. See if you can get Rosalie to help you with that, and then ask her to choose the one she likes the best.'

It had been good advice. Rosalie had selected a pale apple green, which wouldn't have been John's first choice but actually looked very nice when he'd finished. They'd kept going like that and by the end of it Rosalie had a bedroom that she loved, which incorporated all of the things that he'd brought from her room at home, along with a few new things to delight a child, which Cathy had helped him choose.

And now Cathy was gone, leaving behind a devastated husband and two daughters. John had known he couldn't save her, but tried anyway. And all of his own medical training and the quiet assurance of the cardiac specialist who had arrived and made the call that John had been unable to make…none of that was enough to assuage the guilt he'd felt when Cathy's husband had somehow found it in himself to shake John's hand at the funeral, thanking him for doing his best for her.

But he couldn't stop and feel that grief. Just as he'd been unable to stop and feel the grief when his sister had died. As a single mother, his sister Cara had relied on him to help take care of Rosalie and he'd agreed that he would always be there to look after her if anything should happen to Cara. All that mattered to John now was Rosalie's welfare, and falling apart wasn't going to do anyone any good.

Neither would feeling what he imagined he could very easily feel for Reba. He'd learned that lesson when his partner, Elaine, had made him choose between her and adopting Rosalie, throwing in the warning that coping with a child would be impossible while he was settling in to a new promotion at work and grieving for his sister. He had to kiss a sweet goodbye to thoughts of any relationship because even if a partner did accept that he was a single father, it presented a whole new set of possibilities for loss.

His phone rang, and he jumped. The department secretary reminded him that he was late for ward rounds, and John got to his feet. This was what he did best, pushing everything else aside and getting on with the job in hand.

CHAPTER TWO

JOANNE WAS A bright-eyed, energetic young woman, who clearly spent a bit more time than Reba did deciding what to wear every morning. She shook Reba's hand enthusiastically and started off along the corridor at a jaunty pace.

'This is our therapy room. It's all yours for the two days a week that you're here, which are Tuesdays and Fridays, and the other occupational therapists use it at other times.' Joanne opened the door of a large, bright room.

'What happens if someone else wants the room during my two days?' Reba had fallen foul of room allocation systems in various hospitals before now.

Joanne shook her head. 'They can't have it. It's yours. The department secretary's in charge of the rota for all of the therapy rooms, and she sorts out who can have what if someone's sick or on holiday. I heard that there used to be a very complicated system that relied on a mixture of bribery and seniority, but when Dr Thornton took over the department a year ago it was one of the first things he changed.'

'Thanks, that's a relief. And what about the garden outside? Can I use that when I'm working in here?' There was a pair of doors at the far end of the room, leading out into a paved space, shaded by trees and decorated with tubs of flowers. A low brick wall around the perimeter separated the garden from the rest of the hospital grounds.

Joanne grinned suddenly. 'Yes, this area is for the therapists' use. Cathy held sessions out there all the time when the weather was nice. It's away from the wards so you can make some noise without disturbing anyone.'

'That's great, thank you.'

'Over there is your pinboard.' Joanne gestured towards a large, empty pinboard on the wall. 'And here's your cupboard...'

There was something about the way that Joanne ran her hand across one of the two bright posters that decorated the cupboard doors. Reba hesitated.

'These are Cathy's posters?' Even mentioning the previous music therapist's name seemed a little presumptuous, but Joanne had already done so and Reba reckoned it would be all right.

'Yeah. I should have taken them down when

I got everything ready for you, but I left it until later... But this cupboard's yours now.' Joanne began to pick half-heartedly at the sticky tape in the corner of one of the posters.

'Wait... Couldn't we put them somewhere else, maybe on the pinboard?' Reba was new here and she wanted to make her own mark, but sweeping everything of Cathy's away really wasn't the way to go.

'That's a really good idea, but...aren't you going to need all of the space for your notices?'

'I can manage. Do you think it would be nice to keep them?'

'Yes, it would.' Joanne nodded, frowning as she started to peel the sticky tape carefully from the cupboard door. 'This is *your* job though...'

Reba grinned. 'Dr Thornton told me that as well. I appreciate the thought, but I know you're all still thinking of Cathy and my turning up here to replace her can't be easy.'

'He was the one who tried to save Cathy, you know.'

'He did?' Something prickled at the back of Reba's neck.

'Yes, she was sitting in the staff common room, obviously having a cup of tea because it was spilled all over the floor. She had a sudden cardiac arrest. I found her, when I went in to fetch something from my locker...' Joanne's eyes misted suddenly with tears. This couldn't have been the first time that Joanne had spoken about this, but grief required that she repeat it until it hurt a little less.

'I'm so sorry that you had to experience that, Joanne.'

'I ran to find Dr Thornton, but…they said afterwards that she was already gone. He tried CPR anyway… I think we all wanted him to because we couldn't take in what was happening…' Joanne straightened suddenly, wiping her eyes with her hand. 'You don't want to hear about this. Not on your first day.'

The points to note on Reba's list had suddenly become personal. Real people, who cried real tears. Hans would have thrown his arms up in despair at her, but Reba should remember Joanne whenever she was tempted to fall into her father's habit of categorising everything and feeling only the music.

'Thank you for telling me. I can see that this has affected you very deeply.'

Joanne nodded. 'When the cardiac consultant arrived and took over and said…'

'He said that Cathy was gone?' Joanne obviously wanted to talk about this and Reba supplied the words that she seemed unable to say.

'Everyone was really quiet and Dr Thornton was as white as a sheet. I thought he was going to pass out. But suddenly he was organising everything, telling everyone what to do. He took me to his office and gave me a cup of tea, and then called my boyfriend and asked if he could come and take me home.'

'That was kind of him.'

'Yeah. I heard afterwards that he went with the hospital social worker to tell Cathy's family. And he spoke to everyone here as well, telling them what had happened. Most people knew anyway, but he said that he had to speak with everyone so that they got the proper story.'

'Yes, that would have been very important.' And it seemed that none of this had come without a cost, which was written in the creases in John's brow. 'Will you help me with this, Joanne?'

Reba carefully peeled the sticky tape from the cupboard door, carrying the first poster over to the noticeboard that had been assigned to her. When they'd pinned both of the posters up, Joanne smoothing them carefully into place, they took up less than a third of her allotted space.

'There are some things in the cupboard… Tambourines, mostly. Is there anything you've brought with you that you want to put in there?' Joanne fished in her pocket and handed over the key.

'I've got a couple of boxes in my car boot. I'll bring them up later.'

'That's okay, I'll give you a hand carrying them. Then we can go to the wards and I'll introduce you, and then I'll show you the things you really need to know about.' Joanne grinned. 'Ladies' restrooms, and the canteen...'

Joanne's tour had been both thorough and helpful. She'd made a beeline for the people she'd clearly identified as the most helpful on each of the wards, and made introductions. Reba wasn't sure that she'd remember all of the names, but being on smiling terms was a good start. They sat down for lunch together in the canteen, and Reba had decided to ask Joanne one of the questions she'd been saving for John.

'One of the things I like to do if I can is to make music a part of the everyday culture of a department. That's not a part of the therapy that I do but I think it's important.'

Joanne's gaze was animated. 'Because music makes you feel better? That's never a bad thing around here.'

'Yes, exactly. And since today's Friday I thought that I might stay late after work and just play something. It's not a structured thing, more a way of seeing if anyone's interested and comes along.'

'On the violin? What will you play?'

'Anything that anyone wants. Do you have any requests?'

Joanne was obviously thinking about it. 'Dr Thornton would have to give the go-ahead for something like that...'.

'That's where I was hoping you might come in. I was wondering if you might ask him and spread the word a bit. Give me some guidance on how to do it without stepping on anyone's toes. If you have time, that is. I don't want to keep you if there's something else you should be doing.'

Joanne grinned. 'No! Nothing else. Dr Thornton said I should help you settle in.' She picked up her phone from the table. 'I'll see what he says right now...'

First-night nerves. Hans specialised in those, and his process was to hurt feelings and fling anything breakable that came to hand against the wall. Reba preferred the more silent approach, her stomach twisting into knots.

Joanne had been a marvel. She'd not only obtained permission from John, but brought some extra chairs into the therapy room and helped fold and stack the tables against the wall. The door from the corridor was closed so that the work of the hospital wasn't disturbed, and those to the small garden were opened so that people could enter that way. Everything was ready and a cool breeze curled around Reba's shoulders, making her shiver. Hopefully, a room full of people and even some dancing would warm things up.

Joanne appeared in the garden outside, gesturing to her to start playing. Reba raised her violin, feeling the comfort of its touch against her cheek, and sound began to stretch out and fill the empty room. A woman was ushered in from the garden and she beckoned to a man behind her, who was carrying a small boy wearing superhero pyjamas. The family sat down in the far corner of the room and Reba segued into the theme tune from the latest superhero film. The boy grinned, climbing down from his father's lap and inching forward towards her. More people started to arrive and Reba played for each of the children, moving amongst them so that those using wheelchairs weren't left out.

She was starting to enjoy herself now. She played music from cartoons and films, advertising jingles and the choruses of popular songs. Then some tunes to appeal to the adults. She saw Joanne leading a little girl with blonde curls into the room, sitting her down on a chair in the corner and then stopping to smile and listen to the music with her.

Now that people were here and engaged, Reba picked up the pace a little. She played a folk tune that was made for dancing, and feet started to tap. As she played, Reba strolled towards the doors that led out into the garden and Joanne got the message, following her out into the evening sunshine to dance.

Everyone was doing their own thing. A couple of the mums were outside now, dancing with the children, and a nurse was making sure that those who shouldn't be running around stayed sitting, fetching tambourines for those who wanted them. A porter who had brought a little girl seated in a wheelchair made sure that she was comfortable out in the garden space and then executed ballroom dance moves with an imaginary partner, which made everyone laugh.

The little blonde-haired girl was still sitting quietly in the corner, looking longingly out of the window at the people dancing in the garden. She was the only child here who wasn't obviously accompanied by a parent or under the watchful eye of one of the nurses, and Reba caught Joanne's eye and nodded towards the child. Joanne waved, beckoning the little girl to come outside into the garden.

She needed a little encouragement, and Reba walked over to where she was sitting. The music drew her from her chair and the little girl followed her outside and started to dance, her blonde curls bobbing in the sunshine.

'Uncle John!' Her shrill voice made Reba look around as she started to walk back to the group who were sitting inside. 'We're dancing!'

Dr John Thornton was standing in the shade of a tree that spread its branches across the entrance of the garden. He'd clearly come in disguise, because apart from his hair and his clothes nothing about him was the same as the sombre man she'd met.

His grin was all for the little girl, but still it sent a tingle down Reba's spine. He seemed relaxed, his shoulder leaning against the broad trunk of the tree as if he had nothing else to do with the next few minutes but to stay and enjoy. Reba poured all of her own joy into the music, wondering if he might be tempted to join the dancing…

No such luck. But when she moved on to a sea shanty, the rhythm of which reflected the movement of the waves and the *heave-ho* of the hoisting of sails, he started to clap his hands along with everyone else. Little victories.

Joanne caught sight of him and hurried across, clearly worried about what he might think of all of this. A few words, and a smiled retort from John, sent her back to join in with the clapping and the dancing. Reba stationed herself in the doorway between the therapy room and the garden so that she could see everyone and gauge her performance from their reactions.

A quick look at the clock told her that she had time for another dance tune and she chose a pop song this time. Then it was time to slow things down, so that when the children who were on the wards went back they weren't hyped up from all the clapping and dancing. She saw that the little girl had run over to John, and he was sitting on the grass with her.

She should give her attention to everyone equally, even though the pair of them fascinated her. Reba strolled inside, playing as she went, feeling a quiver around her heart that couldn't entirely be put down to the melody she was playing. Even if John was out of sight now he could still hear the music.

At some point, after they'd lost Cathy, John had switched from music radio in the mornings to the sound of muted voices discussing news events that he hadn't bothered to read about in the paper. It was one more step into a world that was quieter and greyer.

He pretended it wasn't happening for Rosalie's sake. But that silent, featureless existence had become a place to retreat to when he was alone. Somewhere he wasn't torn by feelings of guilt and grief, and the endless questions about whether he could have noticed earlier that Cara or Cathy had been ill, and maybe saved either one of them.

He'd intended to just walk down here, make sure that everything was going well and check on Rosalie. But when he saw her, jumping up and down, dancing to the music, he couldn't leave. Rosalie called out to him excitedly and he waved back at her.

Uncle John. Maybe Rosalie did see a difference between the carefree man who'd been her uncle and the one who was now her father, because she didn't often call him *uncle* these days. John stayed beneath the branches of the tree that shadowed the entrance to the garden, watching.

And then he saw Reba. The way she moved, the music and the dancing, seemed to reach out and curl itself around him, leaving him defenceless against the vivid joy that emanated from her.

'Dr Thornton… *Dr Thornton!*' John had been unable to resist clapping along with the music and Joanne brought him back down to earth, a look of worried vigilance on her face. 'What do you think?'

He thought that he wanted to move closer to Reba and touch her. Feel the passion that she harnessed so skilfully. John tore his attention from the dancing and focused on a more acceptable answer.

'It all looks really good. Are you enjoying it?'

'Um…' Joanne shrugged. From the calls he'd received from her during the course of the afternoon, John suspected that Joanne had been so focused on practical preparations that she hadn't reckoned on enjoying this evening.

'All of the patients are supervised?'

Joanne nodded. 'Yes, Reba spoke to the ward manager this afternoon and there are nurses here to keep an eye on things.'

'Then you might like to think about relaxing and joining in now. You've done a really great job with organising this, thank you.' The advice came straight from the mouth of the old Dr John Thornton. The one who had learned how to do his best and then let go of the things he couldn't change.

Joanne grinned suddenly. 'Yes, okay. Thanks, Dr Thornton.'

He could go now. Joanne had walked back to the group of children and was dancing with them. Rosalie seemed to have forgotten he even existed in her excitement. John could go back to his office and finish reading the report he was halfway through…

Suddenly the black and white of print on the page could wait. He wanted this moment for himself. Walking through the gate that led into the garden, John sat down on the grass, watching Reba as she stood in the doorway between the therapy room and the garden. Feeling the glowing exhilaration that he saw on her face. And then the gathering calm as the music began to slow and she segued effortlessly into a slower melody.

Rosalie ran over to him, sitting down on his outstretched legs, her hand tapping his arm in time to the music.

'Enjoying yourself?'

Rosalie nodded. 'Do you like it, Dad?'

'Yes, I do. You want to go home now, or stay until it's finished?'

'Stay!'

Rosalie flung her arms around him as if to make sure he wouldn't move, and John laughed, hugging her back. 'Okay, we'll stay.'

Joanne had insisted on staying to help clear up, and they started to unfold the tables and put them back out, ready for Monday morning. Parents and children were drifting away now and when Reba looked outside John was gone, along with the little girl.

'I saw you talking to Dr Thornton. Was everything okay with him?'

'Yes, he said it all looked really good.'

'The little girl with him seemed to be enjoying herself. That's his niece?' Reba's curiosity got the better of her.

'Yes, Rosalie's his niece. But...' Joanne was interrupted as the last of the parents left the therapy room, calling out a goodbye.

'It was nice to see her joining in with the dancing.' Reba gently steered Joanne back to what she'd been saying.

'Yes, really nice, actually. I'm pretty sure Dr Thornton will give us the go-ahead to do it again.'

'And how about you? Are you okay with that?' It was nice that Joanne already felt involved enough to use the word *us*, and exactly what Reba had hoped to hear.

'Yes, count me in. If you don't mind...'

'Are you kidding? I did the easy bit. You sorted everything out and got everyone to come along.'

Joanne laughed. 'I suppose we make a good team then. I can't play the violin.'

'You've worked really hard to make this a success. Don't you have somewhere to go this evening?' Most people did on a Friday evening. Reba did too, but it was generally home to work out what she might have done better during the week, and how she could correct that next week.

'Everyone's going down to the wine bar for

Lizzie's birthday. You should come, they won't mind if we turn up a bit late.'

'Did you introduce me to Lizzie today?' In the whirl of names and faces, Reba couldn't remember a Lizzie.

'No, but that doesn't matter. It'll give you a chance to get to know everyone.'

'Okay, thanks. Why don't you go now, though? There's not much more to do here, and I'm really grateful for all your help today. I'd hate it if you missed out on some of your evening.'

Joanne paused and then nodded. 'If you don't mind. I'll see you down there then…'

Reba walked back to the hospital car park, deep in thought. One thing about driving home was that she'd been on soft drinks all evening, and sober enough to take in the gossip that had been running around the increasingly unruly birthday celebration.

Lizzie had been opening a stack of birthday cards, reading them all out as she went. There was one from John, and when someone had asked if he was here Reba had heard one of the nurses she'd met earlier bemoaning the fact that he never came to any of these after-work drinks.

'Such a shame. I wouldn't mind getting him drunk one night…'

'Probably why he doesn't come then.' The man sitting next to the nurse chuckled, digging her in the ribs. 'Give him a break, he's a good bloke. Looks after his staff, which is more than some of them do.'

Everyone around the table had nodded in agreement and Reba had stowed the information away for later. It seemed that her own impression, of John's self-contained reserve, was shared by others.

She flipped the remote to unlock her car, and the lights flashed in the darkness. Reba couldn't help being fascinated by John, even if her wish to connect with him, to see him smile, would only distract her from her main purpose. She was here to take on a challenging job, and to succeed. Generally speaking, personal attachments only got in the way of the kind of effort that success demanded.

And she *would* succeed. Hans had taught her that the pursuit of excellence involved single-mindedness, and he was the perfect role model. If he threw things it would be about the music. If he stayed up all night, unable to stop working because something had caught his imagination, it would be about the music. When Hans had shown her love, then that was all about the music that he and Reba shared too.

He'd reacted exactly as Reba had thought he

might when he'd found out about her decision to become a music therapist, telling her that she was wasting her talent. They'd patched things up, but things between them had never been quite the same again, and Reba had channelled all of her energy and single-mindedness into proving him wrong. Maybe if he could have been a fly on the wall at the music evening tonight...

He still would have found her a disappointment. Not as worthy of his love as she had been. Reba had come to terms with that now, but couldn't help feeling that she needed to walk that extra mile to deserve the respect of people around her.

Respect was one thing. An understanding with John, a friendship even, was appropriate and it would help her build on the strong foundations that Cathy had laid. Anything more would be a distraction, which threatened to chip away at what Reba had managed to achieve.

She got into her car, feeling suddenly weary. She'd worked out the one thing that she could have done better this week. Getting through to John might have been her first thought when she'd arrived here, but she should be a little more careful with her emotions next week.

CHAPTER THREE

Tuesday morning. Tuesdays and Fridays were Reba's days, weren't they?

John frowned. Perhaps opening his laptop and taking another shot at the staff roster for next month was a suitable punishment for the thought. Tuesdays and Fridays were music therapy days for his young patients. He really didn't need to think about who was going to be providing the music therapy; all he needed to know was that it was someone who was suitably qualified, and who turned up on the right days.

He'd thought too much about Reba over the weekend, and John had had to remind himself of a few home truths. The days when meeting someone he liked was a simple matter of finding out tactfully whether they felt the same way were long gone. Reba was entrancing, but the life she represented was now lost to him. Just making it through the day, giving Rosalie what she needed and doing what needed to be done here at the hospital was more than enough.

He jumped as a knock sounded on the door of his office. *Now* he was feeling guilty for just thinking about Reba. John rolled his eyes at his own foolishness and waited, and the knock sounded again.

Maybe whoever was outside was carrying something and had their hands full. He got up from his seat, opening the door, and Reba jumped back from it, her eyes flaring in surprise. John realised that he too had started back and that they were now staring at each other.

'Sorry.' Reba was the first to compose herself. 'I didn't hear you call me in.'

'I didn't…' John twisted his lips in what he hoped looked like a suitable smile and not a surprised expression of joy at seeing her so soon after three very long days spent without her. 'Everyone generally just knocks and comes in. If I don't want to be interrupted I'll flip the light on the door, in which case they either come back later or speak to my secretary.'

'Got it… Thanks.' She inspected the small frosted glass panel on the door, which admittedly didn't look too much like an engaged sign when it was off. John walked over to his desk, flipping the remote to activate the panel.

'Oh! Yes, I see. What happens if you're out of your office?'

'The door's locked.'

'Of course it is.' Reba was hovering in the threshold, clearly waiting to be invited in.

'You wanted to speak with me?'

She smiled suddenly. 'Yes, if you have a moment.'

John waved her inside and took refuge behind his desk. Whatever Reba felt, be it joy or uncertainty, the emotion seemed to leak from her, filling the room, and he felt a little more comfortable with a solid barrier between them.

'What did you think of the session on Friday evening?' She didn't wait to get to the question that was obviously on her mind.

'I'd be happy to see it continue, if that's something you'd like to do. I think it will be of benefit.' John closed his mind to the thoughts that crowded in on him. He should forget about the deeply emotional experience of watching Reba play and concentrate on the quantifiable benefits it could bring to the department.

'Was it fun?' She seemed intent on coaxing something more from him.

'My daughter really enjoyed it.' John wondered if it was quite fair to bring Rosalie into it, but he didn't have what Reba seemed to want—couldn't dare to speak about his own reaction.

'The little girl I saw you with? I must have got the wrong idea. I thought someone said she was your niece.'

It would do no harm to explain; everyone here knew what had happened. And his own belief was that the sooner you answered questions honestly, the sooner a difficult subject would go away.

'Rosalie's my adopted daughter. Her mother—my sister—died a year ago.'

Reba's cheeks flushed suddenly, in obvious embarrassment.

'I'm sorry, I didn't mean to...' The look in her eyes said more about compassion than mere words ever could. 'I'm so sorry for your loss. Yours and Rosalie's.'

John nodded the appropriate acknowledgement, trying to distance himself from the feelings involved. 'It was really good to see Rosalie having fun and dancing with the other children. She's still very sad at times.'

'I'm sure she must be. I'm glad she had a good time. If Rosalie would like to come again, I'll make sure to ask her if there's something she'd like me to play...'

'Thank you, I'm sure she'd like that a lot.' John watched as Reba bent, her hair spilling across her shoulders, picking up a large leather handbag and hugging it to her chest. 'Was there something else?'

'Um…no, not really. I just wanted to find out what you thought and ask if it was okay to go ahead and organise another session this Friday evening.'

'Yes, please do.' The words were hardly out of his mouth before Reba got to her feet.

'That's great. Thank you, I'll let you get on.'

Some other emotion that John couldn't define seemed to be pushing Reba on to the next thing on her agenda. She whirled out of his office and John sighed, leaning back in his chair. It seemed that his fascination with Reba just wouldn't let him go, and he was going to have to concentrate a little harder on putting it out of his mind, getting their relationship onto a professional footing, and keeping it there.

Reba was trembling as she walked away from John's office, clutching her bag to her chest. She hadn't shown him the report she'd brought with her, or asked the questions she wanted to ask. She hadn't given the answers she'd prepared to every question he might possibly have asked either.

She walked quickly downstairs to the therapy room, still thinking through the implications of what John had said to her. She knew that he'd been in his current post for a year. And he'd lost his sister a year ago as well, and adopted little Rosalie. Any one of those things was a lot to take on, and all three together...

No wonder he'd retreated behind a wall of professionalism. And when Cathy had died, and John had vainly tried to save her, it must have seemed like the final blow in a whole succession of thunderbolts that had rocked his life.

He'd talked about his sister's death almost as if it had happened to someone else, and it was that disconnection that had shocked Reba the most. In many ways it was admirable that he'd devoted himself so selflessly to his niece and to the department, but he was living in denial and at some point he was going to break.

John Thornton was a man in trouble.

'Not your business, Reba. It's not even close to being your business...' She muttered the words to herself as she opened the music therapy cupboard, sliding the manila envelope that she'd meant to give to John onto one of the shelves. It had felt suddenly unimportant, and it could wait.

What seemed more important was the way that John had reacted to the music on Friday, seeming to relax and spend some time in the moment. Reba hadn't realised quite how precious that was, but she knew now. And she knew that she wasn't just responding to the attraction she felt for him, in wanting to help him.

It wouldn't be easy. Reba's brief conversations with him had given her the distinct impression that John didn't want anyone's help. But not being easy had never stopped her before.

Reba looked at her watch. She had an hour before she was due to see her first patient, and there was work to do.

Little Matthew was her last patient for the morning. He'd been in a car accident, and the resulting head trauma had left him with aphasia, which meant that he couldn't formulate his thoughts into words. Reba knew that she might not be able to help him, but she'd decided that it was worth a try.

'You're on your way to see Matthew? I'd like to join you if I may.' As she approached the four-person ward, John's voice behind her made her jump.

'Of course. Any particular reason?' Reba would actually rather he didn't. John had chosen the patient where she was the least sure of the outcome of her work.

'I'm interested in why you believe Matthew might benefit from music therapy. I thought I might learn something if I kept my eye on this case.'

Was that a nice way of saying that he didn't trust her, and was testing her out? Reba swallowed down her own defensiveness. He wasn't Hans, and he hadn't rejected her for making one decision. But all the same Reba cared what John thought of her and this was unsettling.

She took a breath, stopping and moving to one side in the corridor. It was probably best to have this conversation standing still. 'There's no guarantee of success with Matthew, but I noticed on Friday that he was trying to sing along with the tunes I was playing. I couldn't hear whether he was managing it, so I popped in to the hospital on Sunday, to spend a little time with him.'

'Okay. And what did you find, in this off-duty moment?' There was the trace of a challenge in his tone.

'Walking through the door here makes me on duty,' Reba couldn't help shooting back at him. 'There are documented cases where people with aphasia, who have lost the ability to formulate their thoughts into speech, can respond to music and sometimes even sing.'

'That's not the case for everyone though, is it.'

So this was his issue. It made sense that John might concentrate on numbers and probabilities, in a world where an improbable set of challenges had hit him all at the same time.

'No, but from my observations I think Matthew might. I've spoken to his speech therapist and she's happy for me to do this; she'll be teaching him to slow down and establish a rhythm to help him speak again. I also checked with Dr Curry and she said that it couldn't do any harm.' Matthew's doctor hadn't shown a great deal of enthusiasm for Reba's suggestion, but she hadn't said no either.

'Yes, I spoke with Anna Curry as well. I got the impression that she isn't holding out much hope of this succeeding.' John's expression gave no hint of his own thoughts.

'With all due respect, that's her opinion. If there's a chance I can help Matthew, then I'll take it. Shouldn't we all be taking every chance we have, for each child here…?' Reba pressed her lips together. She'd spoken with Anna Curry without feeling this rush of indignation at her diffidence. Why John?

He held up his hand, as if the feeling in her chest had somehow escaped and was attacking him. 'I agree with you. Anna's an exceptional doctor, but she relies a bit too much on the quantifiable. She'll learn—'

'Music therapy is *not* unquantifiable, John.' Maybe she shouldn't have interrupted him; a brief look of annoyance showed on his face. But somewhere, deep down, even this was welcome because it was an emotion. Any emotion was better than none.

'That's not what I meant. I'm interested in what you're doing with Matthew because I want you to succeed, and I want to learn from that.' He shot her a reproving look, and Reba frowned back at him. He might have said that a bit sooner.

'That's fine, then. You're always welcome at any of my sessions. You're the head of department, after all.' Reba couldn't resist the dig.

'You're not accountable to me. I dare say that the head of therapy will be on my case soon enough if I stand in your way.' John seemed to be intent on splitting hairs, and clearly didn't much mind if she shot back at him. Just as well, because somewhere deep down she wanted this quiet, reserved man to respond to her.

Reba gave a silent nod, ignoring the thought that maybe she was just trying to annoy him now. That should be the end of it, but John seemed in no hurry to get to the ward to see Matthew, stepping out of the way as a porter approached, manoeuvring a bed along the corridor. They had a few more minutes before she was due to collect Matthew and clearly John was thinking of making use of them.

'Would you characterise yourself as ambitious?'

So now he was getting personal. Fair enough.

'I'm ambitious, and I'm not afraid of trying things out. Is there anything wrong with that?'

'No. As long as it works in our patients' favour then I'm all for a little moving and shaking.'

Right now she was moved to shake him. Hard.

'That's what I'd classify as ambition. Going the extra mile to get results for my patients.'

He nodded. 'I'm wondering—do you have anything else up your sleeve in that respect? I've already seen your Friday evening session working well for the children and their parents.'

It had worked well for John as well, although Reba didn't expect him to admit that.

'I have a few ideas. I'll be finished at six this evening; perhaps you have a moment?' Maybe she should have stayed in his office this morning and shown him the document that she'd wanted him to see.

He shook his head. 'Sorry, I'm picking Rosalie up this evening from the nursery. I'll be around on Friday though, and I'm in early most days.'

'No problem. I'll catch you then.' Reba looked at her watch again, in an indication that they'd be late for Matthew if they didn't go to the ward soon, and he nodded. As she started to walk, she thought she heard John murmur that he'd be looking forward to it.

Matthew's other injuries from the accident included a broken leg, and he was already in a wheelchair and waiting for his therapy session when they arrived in the four-bed ward. Beckoning to her, the senior nurse gave her a list made by Matthew's mother, noting down all his favourite songs. Reba stopped to ask a couple of questions about how Matthew had been since she'd last seen him, standing so that she could keep an eye on what John was up to.

He walked over to Matthew, squatting down on his heels in front of him. The boy grinned and gave him a wave, and John spoke to him quietly, waiting for Matthew's nod of agreement before he released the brakes on the wheelchair, bringing him over to where Reba was standing.

'Hey Matthew. Are you ready to come and do some work with me?' Reba waited. Giving Matthew time and showing that she was interested in his reactions, however he was able to express them, was important.

Matthew nodded, returning her smile.

'Right then. Shall we go?'

If the thought of working under John's watchful gaze was confronting, the reality wasn't so bad. He sat quietly in one corner of the therapy room, leaving her to start the process of singing the chorus of one of the songs on the list, to see how Matthew reacted. With a little practice and a great deal of encouragement, Matthew was able to reproduce the tune, and then a couple of indistinct words.

'That's really great, Matthew. Well done.' It took a great deal of effort on Matthew's part to do just this, and he needed all of the praise he could get.

'Nice one. Fantastic.' John added his own encouragement.

It was the first—no, the second time that Reba had seen him really smile. Rosalie had brought that sudden grin to his face, and it had made Reba's knees go weak then too. Perhaps you had to be five years old, or in Matthew's case eight, to get the benefit of it.

It was just as well that he saved the tight-lipped, insincere looking ones for her. That way he could be classed as handsome but a little uptight. Goodness only knew how her already raging pheromones would react if she was the target of the encouragement that he was currently aiming at Matthew.

She was just contemplating the thought when John got to his feet. 'I'm looking forward to hearing what you have to say for yourself in the coming weeks, Matthew. Keep going, eh?'

Matthew nodded and gave him a thumbs-up. John nodded at her and walked quickly from the room, leaving her thumping heart a little time to return to something approaching normal.

'Okay. Shall we try that again, Matthew...?'

CHAPTER FOUR

Reba was good at her job. She was patient and kind, giving Matthew exactly the kind of firm encouragement that he needed. When John had looked through the notes she'd written in preparation for joining the therapy team, it was clear that Reba was planning on involving herself in all aspects of the department's work. Comforting children and helping them to express their fears, through playing or song-writing. Making herself available to attend physical and speech therapy sessions, if the relevant therapists felt that she could help out there.

Cathy would have liked her. A lot. Even though Reba's approach was slightly different to hers, Cathy would have felt that the job she was so committed to was in good hands. And she would have admired Reba's passion...

And why would her passion be such a problem to you, John? He could practically see the twinkle in Cathy's eye as he imagined her asking the obvious question.

Because passion wasn't a part of his life any more. He'd taken on a new job that carried heavy responsibility soon after a bereavement and the adoption of a child. That was enough for anyone.

'You don't have anything to prove, John...'

Cathy had said that more than once to him, adding her gentle smile to the mix to soften the blow of truth. Because he *did* have something to prove. Elaine had left him because he couldn't turn away from Rosalie, telling him that he couldn't manage this along with a new job, and she wasn't going to watch him try.

In his own mind, John had questioned whether that was just Elaine's excuse—a reason to stop him from adopting a child—because she'd never questioned it when he'd accepted the new job. But all the same the suggestion had rankled. He knew he could be a good father to Rosalie, and that was what his sister had wanted. He knew that he could take this new job on, carefully ironing out all of the idiosyncrasies that had developed over the years, under a head of department who judged his staff in terms of their expressions of loyalty to him rather than their ability to do their jobs.

And he'd done it.

At a cost, John. If you can't give yourself time to grieve, then you can't move on. And if you don't move on then how can you feel passion...?

Enough! If he wanted to honour Cathy's memory, then stopping having imaginary conversations with her in his office would be an excellent first step. John snapped his laptop closed, tucking it under his arm and grabbing his jacket.

He needed to stop thinking about how Reba's passion had awakened a restless yearning in his own heart and get on with his life. Tonight was pizza night with Rosalie, and arranging smiley faces to eat with his daughter would fix everything.

Why wasn't he surprised to hear a knock on his office door at five past seven on Friday morning? Generally speaking, anyone who worked days and came in this early would be carving out some time to get on with something uninterrupted, and those who worked nights wouldn't be off shift yet. Obviously Reba didn't feel the need to conform to those expectations, and John couldn't help a quickly concealed smile as she burst into his office.

'You wanted to run something past me?'

'Yes. If you have a moment.'

He nodded, motioning her towards one of the

chairs on the other side of his desk. Reba took possession of it, and John wondered whether she ever did anything as mundane as just sitting down. Whenever he found himself in her presence, Reba seemed to become the centre of everything. He watched her push her hair back, his gaze running along the curve of her cheek before he remembered not to stare. Reba pulled a manila envelope from her bag, sliding it across his desk.

'This document's just a draft. It's a few ideas, intended to open a conversation about how I might further develop music therapy services in the department. I was wondering if you might get a chance to look it over.'

'Yes, of course. I'd be very interested to see what your thoughts are.'

When he opened the envelope there were two bound copies of the report inside, their thickness telling him instantly that this was probably more than just a few ideas. It didn't look much like a draft either, on the front a vivid design, featuring line drawings of musical instruments and a wash of coloured shapes that curled and blended together like a melody. Reba had obviously put some work into the presentation, and John opened the top copy, scanning the contents page.

'There's a lot here. You're going to have to

give me a chance to read this through carefully, but I'll give it my full attention and let you know what I think. Then perhaps we can set up a meeting with the head of therapy—I assume he'll have the last word on this.'

Reba scrunched up her face. John wondered if he'd innocently managed to put his finger on one of the hurdles that she had undoubtedly anticipated.

'The thing is… I gave him a copy of a document very much like this, which was a set of boilerplate ideas taken from my past experience and…he said he liked the look of some of them and I should update it with particular reference to *this* department once I'd got my feet under the table. Then give it to you…'

John was tempted to ask whether Reba really felt she'd got her feet under the table yet, when from what he'd seen she hardly ever even sat down. Even now she was shifting in her seat as if she'd rather be moving. But that would be a little too personal, and probably annoying.

'I see. You're in a position where neither of us will actually take responsibility for doing anything about your ideas.' He saw a flicker of something that looked like a frustrated *yes* on her face. 'In that case leave this with me. I'll take responsibility for it and come back to you with a solid response.'

She puffed out a breath. 'Thank you. I really appreciate that. And you're willing to put some of my ideas into practice?'

He hadn't even read her report yet, and until he had John should manage her expectations. 'Give me time to find out what they are first. And I'll tell you now that I don't intend to implement any changes without first discussing the implications with everyone involved in patient care here. And that's going to take time.'

'So…more red tape.' Reba shot him a look that suggested he was trying to strangle her with it. If he didn't know better John would have reckoned that Reba's ambition was making her forget what she was here for.

But he'd seen her with Matthew. And he'd heard the reports of doctors and ward managers that he trusted, and if Reba's approach was sometimes a little unorthodox it was always patient-centred and effective.

And he could feel a perverse, overpowering desire to see her stop looking so dejected and fight him. If he couldn't contemplate her passion in any other part of his life, it might be okay to allow himself a taste of it here, in the safety of his office.

'There's always red tape. Surely you know that.'

She frowned at him. 'But… John, my ideas

are good. They're not just something I've plucked out of the air; they're backed up by my experience and other people's research.'

'And I have to make sure that we can implement them well.'

'I know that but…' Reba finally got to her feet, seeming suddenly to regain her rhythm as she paced back and forth. 'This isn't just about solid therapeutic principles, it's about delight. Making people smile and find a way to face what's coming next. We *all* need to do that, don't we?'

Was the smiling and facing what came next aimed solidly at him? Irrespective of Reba's intentions, John felt it like a blow to the chest.

'We need to do our jobs, Reba. You know full well that isn't all about delight.' He struck back unthinkingly now, hurt by the idea that Reba might think he wasn't coping.

'But you're happy for this evening to go ahead, at least?'

He'd already said yes. And he really didn't want to think any more about the feelings that last Friday night had engendered. The way he'd wanted to touch her, to feel the passion that she harnessed with such skill.

'I've given you my answer on that.'

'Thank you.'

Something about the way she marched back

to the chair she'd been sitting in to fetch her handbag told him that her thanks were just another weapon in Reba's arsenal. John ignored the gesture, putting the reports into his in-tray with rather more of a flourish than he'd intended.

But Reba was clearly not finished with him yet. She got halfway to the door and then whirled round, her hair flying in synchronicity with the movement, in an expression of something that tore at his heart. A fluidity of emotion that he'd lost somewhere along the way.

She wasn't thinking any more, she was simply doing. A force of nature, seeming to bear down on him like a hurricane. This was the Reba he'd seen on Friday, who'd captured everyone's hearts with her music.

John moved back as she leaned over his desk. There was no arguing with a hurricane, it just went its own way and blew itself out when it was ready.

'I was taught never to walk away from a disagreement. Throw something, get it out of your system and move on.'

Ripping the blank sheet of paper from the pad in front of him, she screwed it up into a ball and threw it. It hit the wall and dropped into the wastepaper bin. Good shot.

'Am I supposed to take that as a peace offering?' John unsuccessfully tried to keep himself from smiling. If he engaged with this any more than he already had, who knew how else he might be tempted to engage with Reba?

'No. You can take it as a temporary respite. I'm not going to give up on this, John.' She jutted her chin towards him.

John met her gaze. 'Good. Looking forward to that.'

Her scent lingered for a moment as she left the room. Not *quite* slamming the door behind her, but John jumped anyway.

He stared at the door, wondering whether she'd be back with any last words for him. Hoping she might but wishing she wouldn't, all at the same time. His heart was pounding in his chest, and if the room seemed to have escaped any permanent disruption, he certainly hadn't.

John pinched the bridge of his nose, wondering whether he shouldn't have just taken the report, thanked her and left it at that. But something told him that none of this was about the things they'd acknowledged. It was about the clash of unacknowledged passion that seemed to hover in the air whenever they came within fifty feet of each other.

He was going to have to stop thinking with his heart and start using his head. Wanting to see Reba again, and indulge in throwing a few more things around with her, wasn't going to help in terms of getting things done today. And getting through the day, doing his job and keeping Rosalie safe and happy, was all that he could realistically expect at the moment.

Reba wanted to lock herself away in the therapy room and hide. What on earth had she been thinking? Throwing things, even if a balled-up piece of paper, couldn't do any damage. Practically declaring war on the head of department...

The answer was that she *hadn't* been thinking. She'd acted with her emotions, and that was never a good idea. She knew as well as John did that change took time, discussion and, most of all, a light touch. She'd never clashed with anyone, or pushed for her ideas to be heard like this. The report she'd written had been intended to support her application for this job and show that she did have ideas, and it had been the head of therapy who'd suggested that she pass it on to Dr Thornton when she felt the time was right.

But suddenly it had become important to her. She'd worked all weekend and a couple of evenings this week, updating and perfecting it. Reba really didn't want to think about what had driven her to do that, but she couldn't help it. Growing up with Hans, she'd learned that love was inextricably linked with achievement. And she'd found herself pushing to achieve something that really should have waited, in order to gain John's approval.

She wondered briefly whether John would raise her behaviour this morning with the head of therapy, and dismissed the thought. It hadn't taken long for her to find out that everyone in the department reckoned him to be an honest and fair boss. All the same, it would be best if she kept her head down for a little while. And maybe she could just hold on to a little of that warm, reassuring hope that John would like some of the ideas she'd presented…

It had been a busy day, and Reba was tired. Maybe that was why these second-night nerves felt more acute than the first-night ones had been. She'd seen John a couple of times as she'd moved around the department today and each time he'd acknowledged her with a smile, which Reba had quickly returned. It seemed that he'd taken her suggestion of moving on at face value, and she was grateful for that and didn't want anything to go wrong tonight.

It was a warm evening and Reba opened the doors into the garden, her stomach twisting into knots as she saw John walking towards her with Rosalie. The little girl was jumping up and down in excitement and John let go of her hand, letting her run ahead of him into the garden.

'Hi Rosalie. Are you coming for the music?'

Rosalie nodded, suddenly shy.

'I was hoping you'd be here. It wouldn't be the same without you. Would you like to choose a song for me to play?'

'Yes!'

Reba chuckled. 'Okay, you think about what you want and make sure to come and tell me.'

'Thank you.' John had caught up with his daughter, and when Reba looked up at him he was smiling.

'It's my pleasure.'

'Hey Rosalie.' Joanne appeared at the doors into the garden, holding a large carrier bag. After greeting Rosalie she beckoned to Reba, who left John and his daughter alone for a moment.

'What do you think? I went to my cousin's little girl's birthday party at the weekend and these were left over.'

Reba reached into the bag, drawing out a sparkly wand from the pile. 'They're brilliant!' She grinned, tapping Joanne on the head with it. Joanne laughed, mimicking a sudden transformation into a princess.

'And there are some fairy lights. They're

the old ones from our tree, but I got them PAT tested and they work fine.'

'Joanne, you're a marvel. Thank you.' Reba felt a small body leaning against her leg and looked down to see Rosalie, her eyes fixed pleadingly on the sparkly wand she was holding. Joanne laughed, leading her away to choose her favourite from the bag.

When she'd started playing all of her fatigue and worry had disappeared. Reba had seen John on the outskirts of the group, circulating amongst the parents and children. Talking to everyone, joining in, but somehow still as separate from everyone as he always was.

The reserved smile gave it away. John was very definitely still at work.

Still buzzing from the music, she took the opportunity of John standing alone for a moment to approach him.

'What did you think?'

His smile faded suddenly, and that was something of a relief. Reba wanted his opinion, not pleasantries.

'I see you've been putting your own principles into practice. Letting people contribute and feel ownership, and allowing it to grow organically. When I spoke to Anya, she said she'd heard about this on the grapevine and decided

to come along and see what it was all about.' He
nodded towards the receptionist for the department, who'd collected her two-year-old from the
hospital nursery and brought him along.

'You thought I'd been persuading people to
come?'

John nodded. 'It had occurred to me. Clearly
I was wrong, this seems to be gaining its own
momentum.'

No smiles. If anything there was an under-
tone of hostility between them, but John had
kept an open mind and was being honest with
her. That seemed more intimate than anything
else he'd done so far this evening.

'I stick to what my experience tells me will
work. The same as you do.'

'What happens when you find you have more
people than you can handle?'

'I don't think that'll be an issue for a while.
I'm expecting fewer people once the novelty
wears off. We'll deal with that if it happens. I'm
sure you've gathered from my report that I ad-
vocate a very flexible and responsive approach
to this kind of activity.' She let him know that
she'd noticed he'd read at least some of the report that she'd given him this morning.

'Right, then. Well, have a good weekend...'

'You too. Thank you, John.'

His impassive nod was better than even the

real smile that he gave when he looked around for Rosalie, calling to her that it was time to go now. Reba watched him walk away holding Rosalie's hand, his head bent towards his daughter's excited chatter.

John was a challenge. She'd always known he would be, but so far he'd managed to surpass even her wildest dreams. But she knew now that she could meet that challenge, although Reba wasn't sure what the cost might be.

CHAPTER FIVE

TUESDAY MORNING. Two whole days at the weekend to think and prepare for the week ahead. She knocked on John's door at half past eight in the morning, and saw him look up from his laptop screen as she entered.

'You're late this morning.'

She reckoned he was referring to her presence in his office rather than what time she'd entered the building. Reba ignored the comment and laid the leaflets she'd printed at the weekend in front of him on his desk. John glanced at them and nodded.

'They look nice. Do I have anything to worry about?'

'Not if you don't mind orange.' The image on the front was an adaptation of the one that adorned the report she'd given him, and Reba had wondered on her way up here whether she'd overdone the bold orange splash of colour at the centre of the image.

'Nope. Orange is good.' He gestured towards the chair opposite him and opened the trifold leaflet. Reba watched him as he read the contents of it carefully.

'Looks good. I like your idea of making it a personal invitation to the Friday music evening. I assume you're intending to write each child's name inside.'

'Yes, that's the idea. Is it okay if I give some to each of the ward managers, so they can distribute them as they see fit?'

John saw straight through the question. 'You're asking me? You're at liberty to spread the word about any of your agreed activities.'

'I know you're watching what I do, John.'

He leaned back in his seat, the flicker of a smile on his face. 'Fair enough. I think it's a good idea to have the ward managers decide whether a child or their parents should be given an invitation. They see everyone and not just the children who are referred to you. Is that okay?'

'It'll do.' Reba returned his look of amused confrontation, feeling a quiver of excitement in her stomach. It was good to see him after three days spent thinking about him. And *really* good that he'd liked what she'd done.

She took the leaflet from his grasp, writing his and Rosalie's names into the box intended for that purpose. Then she handed it back to him.

'Thanks. Anything else?'

'No, that's all for this morning.' Reba was going to quit while she was ahead this time.

'Okay. By the way, I finished reading your report over the weekend, and I'm just going through it again to add a few comments. You're free on Friday morning some time?'

Just when she was feeling in control of the situation. John really did know how to command the last word.

'Half seven?'

He nodded. 'Yep, I'll have my response ready by then. Look forward to discussing it with you.'

Reba had endured the pleasures of seeing John during the course of the day on Tuesday, telling herself that she could handle the way his grey-blue eyes always seemed a lot bluer when he smiled. The thrill she felt whenever she saw him, and the way she wanted to touch him.

She'd spent Thursday evening, and a large part of the following night, trying not to worry about John's reaction to her report and failing spectacularly. After four hours' sleep, she assessed the queue at the hospital coffee shop and decided that she didn't have time to order and get upstairs for seven-thirty.

'I suppose if we're both late then neither of us is.' She heard John's voice behind her.

'Hmm. Logical.' Reba joined the queue with him. He somehow managed to manoeuvre his way in front of her before they got to the cash desk, and paid for her coffee. Reba smiled a thank you, allowing herself to think of this as a kind gesture from a man she was beginning to like a lot. As long as she kept the lust out of it, that was appropriate.

They walked up to his office together, managing to keep the obligatory conversation about how the last few days had gone for each of them to the minimum, since it appeared they'd done much the same as they always did. Reba had worked, and John had got by. But they sat down on either side of his desk with a little more relaxed joviality than was usual between them.

'I was really impressed by your report.' He started off with a smile. 'I've made a few notes in the margins but they're really just points for discussion.'

John reached into his briefcase, taking out one of the copies of the report and leaning across to hand it to her. Reba took it and opened the front cover, leafing through.

His bold, clear handwriting was everywhere. Questions, points to consider…even a few remarks about passages that he particularly liked.

John had been through everything she'd done with the same meticulous care that Hans took…

She should be pleased. She should thank him for the time he'd taken to do this. But all that Reba could think was that a man she cared about had applied his talent and knowledge to something she'd done. With that came the possibility of rejection and disappointment.

She blinked away the tears, making sure that John didn't see them. Took a sip of her coffee in the hope that it would steady her a bit, but it didn't.

'Thank you. I'm going to have to take some time to read all of this, but I really appreciate your having given it all such careful consideration.' She'd stopped to read some of the points that John had made, and they were good ones.

'My pleasure.' He seemed to have noticed her discomfiture. 'I hope you understand that my motives are to try and make this all happen, and not to throw a spanner into the works.'

That just made it worse. If he'd been a little more confrontational about it, Reba could have dealt with that. She knew how to stand up to John, and that he didn't react badly to her doing so. As a matter of fact, there seemed to be times when he enjoyed it as much as she did.

'Yeah… Yes, I understand. Thank you.' Reba gathered her bag and coat, getting ready to leave.

An hour on her own, reading through his comments and convincing herself that this was all okay, and then things would seem a lot different.

'There was one other thing…that I wanted to raise with you personally.' The sudden crease in his brow told Reba that he was no more at home with the idea than she was.

'Of course…' She steeled herself for whatever was coming.

'I'm very happy for you to involve others in this but I have two concerns. Firstly that you're not asking people in the department to do more on top of their already considerable workload.'

Reba breathed a sigh of relief. She could answer that. 'That's not my intention at all. If anyone wants to come to something they're welcome. I'm going to be the one doing all the work.'

'It's a lot for just one person. From what I've seen already, you're spending a great deal of time on this.'

'It won't take any time away from my clinical work with patients.' Reba had learned all about commitment from Hans, and there was no such thing as skimping in one area to give time to another.

'That wasn't something that occurred to me. I'm just concerned that you're using too much of your own time on this.'

Pastoral care? Probably not. John knew exactly how things worked. These were questions he might ask his own staff, but if they were asked of her they'd be asked by the head of therapy. This was different, one friend caring about another. That was the part that really hurt.

Leave. Now. Give him some empty reassurance that this really didn't take as long as it sounded, which would get the message across that what she did with her time outside the hospital wasn't any of his concern.

Reba stayed in her seat. 'John, there's something I want to say.'

'Yes?'

'*You* need a break. Maybe music isn't your thing, but you need to let off a bit of steam.'

His face was suddenly blank, devoid of any emotion. This was exactly what she was talking about…

'I'll take that under advisement.'

'No, you won't.' Anger…passion…maybe a mix of the two began to rage in her chest. 'You're clearly tired and you've given so much that you don't have much more to give. What happens when there's nothing left?'

Something stirred in his face. The same kind of dangerous passion that she felt. They'd been playing with fire, allowing competitiveness and confrontation to shape their relationship. Reba had been using it as a barrier to contain her raging feelings, and she should have known that was never going to work, because it had slipped so easily into open confrontation.

'Thanks for the advice. But aren't you crossing a line here?'

That was the last straw. He'd started this.

'Yes, I'm crossing a line. One that you've drawn because you won't take anything from anyone here, because you're the boss and you're supposed to look after everyone else. Well, you're not *my* boss and so I'm going to tell you what everyone else can't.' The words came out in a mess of emotion.

'So now we're getting down to it, are we? You've decided to make a project out of me?' He got to his feet, raw power seeming to emanate from him. It sent shivers down Reba's spine. 'That's up to you, but I can tell you now that I'm not a willing participant, and frankly it's a bit of an insult.'

'There's no insult intended. I see what I see and I'm concerned. As a...'

Colleague? Not really. She wasn't strictly part of his department. Friend? She'd known him for two weeks. Someone who felt drawn into caring about him? Too embarrassing to admit.

'...as a musician.' Reba frowned. That wasn't it either.

Something seemed to break inside him, and he threw up his hands. His frustration washed over her like a great, exciting wave.

'Right. So you play a few well-chosen tunes, and everyone flocks to your bidding. Who are you, the Pied Piper of Hamlyn?'

'No! That's not what I mean at all.' She'd meant that she dealt in emotion. Not necessarily the kind of passion that seemed to be escaping from both of them now, hitting the walls with such force she could almost feel them shake. She didn't fully understand this desperate, glorious overreaction. It came from a connection she felt with John that was far too complicated to name.

'Then what do you mean, Reba?' He planted his hands on his desk, leaning forward. 'Just tell me now so that I know what to expect and I can make arrangements to avoid it.'

As if she was going to back off now. The other side of his desk was a step away and she took it, staring him down. Staring at least because neither of them was going to give way and she would have been disappointed if John had.

'I mean that I'm a therapist. I'm trained to recognise the signs when someone's in emotional overload and I'm trained to offer help if I can.'

'Thanks for the offer, then. I'll decline...' He

gritted the words out. 'And, by the way, I'm a doctor. I'm trained to recognise the signs when someone's in physical overload. You're excellent at your job, but sometimes you need to know when to let go of it and take some time for yourself. You want some help with that?'

Clearly that wasn't an offer. 'I work hard. I'm not ashamed of it. When did that hurt anyone?'

He rolled his eyes. 'You really want me to make a list of the kinds of things that happen when you don't get a break?'

They'd worked their way round in a circle. The only thing left to do was to forget their differences and channel that passion into something a little more intimate, or leave. Turning quickly, Reba grabbed her jacket and bag and headed for the door.

'Go ahead and make that list, John. You might see something there that strikes a chord and, who knows, you might even take the wild step of following your own advice, since you don't seem to want to listen to anyone else.'

She slammed the door behind her. Reba wasn't a big fan of slamming doors, she'd heard enough of that when she was a child, but sometimes it was just something you had to do.

Reba. Reba…

This had been inevitable from the first moment he'd seen her. Everything had been leading up to this sudden loss of control. John turned from his desk, pacing for a while like a caged animal. Then he took a couple of breaths.

The smile when he thought of her face, bright with anger and even more beautiful, wasn't appropriate. Nor was the way he'd wanted to follow her, catch her arm and make her see him. Make her understand the hurt he felt, in the hope that she might battle it on his behalf. She didn't need to be gentle with him—plenty of other people had tried gentle and failed. What he needed was a raging warrior, and he saw that in Reba's eyes.

He heard a knock on his door and jumped. John looked around his office to see if there were any signs of the battle that had taken place, before smiling at Joanne.

'Hey. You're early.'

'Yes, I decided to do eight until four today, so I'd have some time to help Reba with the music tonight. If that's okay...'

'Of course. As long as you're here during your core time that's entirely up to you.' The office staff were on flexi-hours and expected to work an eight-hour day and be in the office between ten and four. 'You seem to really enjoy it.'

Joanne smiled. 'Yes, I do. It's nice to let off

a bit of steam at the end of the week, and I like seeing the children enjoy themselves.'

John nodded. Joanne very clearly wanted to do this, and felt under no pressure. 'What was it that you wanted?'

'Did you get a chance to sign those timesheets I passed over to you yesterday?'

They could have waited. Perhaps Joanne had really popped in to show him that she was here, so that he wouldn't question it if she wasn't at her desk after four o'clock. He grinned at her, feeling an inexplicable impulse to laugh. As regrettable as his shouting match with Reba had been, there was something about her passion that always made him feel alive.

'Sit down, I'll do it now.' John reached for the folder on his desk, flipping through the admin timesheets and signing them all, pausing when he got to Joanne's.

'This is a timesheet, Joanne. Not a work of fiction.'

Joanne's eyes widened in alarm. 'What's wrong with it?'

'You've put down nine till five for the Friday before last. You were at the admin meeting at eight in the morning, and you didn't leave until well after six-thirty that evening.'

'Oh.' Joanne was clearly pleased that he'd noticed. 'Well, yes, but that was Reba's first music session, and I was helping during the afternoon as well. So it kind of evens up, doesn't it?'

'No, it doesn't. I assigned you to helping Reba with whatever she needed that day, and when you came to me to get my go-ahead for the evening session I distinctly remember asking if you wouldn't mind keeping an eye on how it was all going.' He gave Joanne a kindly smile, to fix it clearly in her mind that this wasn't a telling-off.

'I have to put that down then?'

'For that day, yes. If you want to continue to go to the sessions, for your own enjoyment, then you can give it a miss on the timesheet. Does that sound fair?'

'Yes...' Joanne leaned over, grabbing the timesheet and carefully altering it, adding her initials to the amendments.

'Thank you.' John took the timesheet back and scribbled his signature at the bottom. 'Don't think I don't notice how conscientious you are about your work, Joanne.'

'Thanks...' Joanne was positively glowing with pleasure now. She seemed to be reacting far better than Reba had to the suggestion that she make more of a distinction between work and free time, although John had to admit that age, seniority and the fact that it was his business to look out for everyone in the department might have something to do with that.

'Is Rosalie coming along tonight? I can take her if you're busy. Unofficially, of course.'

John chuckled. 'That's really kind of you. I do have to work but my parents' regular Friday night dinner has been cancelled for this week, so my mother's going to bring her. I appreciate the offer though. Thank you for thinking of Rosalie.'

'Right then. Well, I'll look forward to seeing her and…' Joanne picked up the folder from his desk. 'Better get on.'

'Yep. Have a good day, Joanne.'

'Oh. Yes, you too…' Joanne bounced out of the room, grinning.

John leaned back in his seat, putting his hands behind his head. Maybe Reba did have a point about him needing to let off steam a bit from time to time. The whole episode had been frustrating, enraging and painful, and his first impulse was to try and forget all about it. But however challenging the truth was, it was still the truth.

CHAPTER SIX

REBA HADN'T SEEN John all day. Maybe she could just avoid him for a while, and pretend that what had happened this morning was all part of the only half-serious confrontations they'd had up till now. That didn't seem like a way forward. The sudden explosion had been waiting to happen, and neither of them could back away from it now.

Meanwhile she could concentrate on the here and now, and playing for whoever chose to attend the music hour. Reba closed her eyes, her fingers on the neck of her violin, going through the mental exercises she used to focus herself. They didn't seem to be working quite as well as they usually did.

A banging sounded on the doors that led out into the walled garden. Reba opened her eyes and saw Rosalie, pressing her nose against the glass. Sudden joy made her catch her breath. John had decided to come tonight.

Or…not. As she opened the door and Rosalie rushed inside she saw an older woman hurrying to catch up with her.

'Rosalie…' The woman gave Reba an apologetic smile. 'I'm sorry. Rosie and I were just looking for the music session. I suppose we must be in the right place.' She gestured towards Reba's violin.

'Yes, you are. You're the first to arrive.'

'Is it all right if we join in? I'm Babs Thornton, Rosalie's grandmother.'

She could see the resemblance now. Babs had the kind of ready smile that Reba reckoned John might have if he actually allowed himself to express any emotion without thinking about it first, and the same grey-blue eyes.

'Of course, everyone's welcome. I'm so pleased that you came.'

'Rosalie hasn't stopped talking about it and John tells me you've done a marvellous job…'

Had he, now? Reba felt her ears begin to redden. Interrogating his mother about what else he might have said was tempting but a very bad idea, and she made do with a smile and a thank you.

'This is Reba, Grandma.' Rosalie had come to rest beside her grandmother. 'I help her play the violin.'

Babs smiled, winking at Reba. 'Well, that's

very good of you, Rosalie.' She held out her hand and Reba took it. Babs' handshake was surprisingly firm and businesslike.

'Now, we'd better give these to Reba, eh, Rosalie...' Babs reached into the bag she was carrying and produced two tins, giving the smaller one to Rosalie to hand over.

'Cakes! Thank you so much, they're beautiful!' The tin contained a dozen iced fairy cakes.

'There are more in here...' From the weight of the second tin, Babs had clearly made sure that there would be enough for everyone. 'The rather dodgy decorations are mine and the nice ones are Rosalie's.'

'I'll go and see if I can find a plate for them.'

'Oh, don't worry about that. I'm sure people can manage to take them out of the tins. I stopped off at the staff canteen and swiped some serviettes.' Babs produced a packet from her bag. 'I used to work here, so they know who I am.'

'What did you do?' This felt like going behind John's back and asking about his private life, but Babs had proffered the information and it seemed rude not to show some interest.

'I was a neurologist. John dallied with the idea of neurology when he was at medical school, but then he rotated to Paediatrics and after that it was all he ever wanted to do.' Babs' gaze focused over Reba's left shoulder and she turned to see Matthew and his mother in the doorway.

She whispered an, 'Excuse me,' to Babs, and went over to greet them.

'Are we too early?' Matthew's mother looked around the room.

'No, we'll be getting started very soon. Hello, Matthew…'

Matthew responded with a thumbs-up, and Reba smiled, shaking her head. Raising her violin, she played the chords that Matthew had been practising his hellos to.

Matthew replied with not just a hello but the words *music* and *mum* to indicate why he and his mother were here.

'That's brilliant, Matthew. Well done.' Reba grinned at his mother. One of the best things about helping a child to speak again was to see their parents' faces when they first started to say *Mum* and *Dad*.

'Wonderful!' Reba turned to see Babs' hand flying to her mouth. 'Sorry. Force of habit. Not interfering… Rosalie, shall we go and sit down now?'

Babs and John had survived the same tragedy but it appeared they'd done it in different ways. Reba decided not to ponder on that too much and saw Matthew's mother going over to the corner where Babs was now sitting, obviously introducing herself. Babs made room for Matthew's wheelchair and the two women sat chatting together as Rosalie ran over to Joanne, who was shepherding some of the unit's young patients into the room.

It was chillier this evening and the senior nurse had recommended they stay inside. Joanne helped give out the percussion instruments from the cupboard and Reba concentrated on getting the children to play this time. She knew some of her patients' favourite songs now, and when she played Matthew's she saw him nodding to the music, his lips moving as if he was trying to sing. Babs leaned towards him to listen, giving his mother an encouraging nod and a smile…

Everyone had gone home. It had been a good evening. The parents were getting to know each other and the children knew that they could request their favourite songs. Reba had finished off as usual by slowing down the pace, and after the children were back in their wards some of the parents stayed to chat together. This was one of the things that Reba had hoped would happen, that people would start making connections with each other.

She sat on the wall that divided the small

therapy garden from the rest of the hospital grounds, wrapped in the large woollen jacket she kept in the car. Lights glimmered from the wards through bright patterned curtains, and on the top floor of the long three-storey building she could see the light in John's office, becoming brighter by the minute as dusk fell.

She saw him at the window, looking out and stretching his arms. The bright shadow of a man who seemed to haunt her every waking moment. Reba froze, hoping that she was hidden amongst the dark, anonymous shapes of the trees. John seemed to look down for a moment, but then turned away from the window.

Ten minutes later she was still there, still pondering the events of today. John's light flipped off and the slim connection that seemed to bind them keeping her out here in the darkness, snapped. She should go home, pour herself a glass of wine, try to forget about the mistakes she'd made, which hadn't seemed like mistakes at all when she was making them…

That was probably the definition of a mistake. Something that seemed like a good idea at the time but turned out not to be. A cool breeze moved in the trees and she shivered, wrapping her jacket around her a little more tightly.

The door from the therapy room opened and closed behind her. John walked out into the gar-

den, swinging his long legs over the wall and
sitting down, a full two metres away from her.

'I should apologise. But—'

Reba shook her head. 'It's me that needs to
apologise.'

John thought for a moment, staring into the
darkness. 'Can either of us say that we're not
planning on doing this again? An apology's no
good without that.'

'No. I can't.'

Their mutual attraction—Reba knew that
John felt it too—and their confrontational style.
The passion of an argument was only ever the
quickening of a heartbeat away.

'Are you free on Sunday?'

Reba stared wordlessly at him. Even now,
with the light shining across his face, John was
impossibly attractive. Magnetic even, because
magnets had the power to attract and repel with
equal force.

'You've booked brainwashing sessions for us
both?' She ventured a joke and he smiled suddenly.

'I reckoned that might be the measure of last
resort. I was thinking lunch, at my place. Me
and Rosalie. It's a little late to ask but if you
don't have anything planned...'

Okay. Rosalie was the first thing to note
about the invitation. Her presence would stop

anything adult, such as a passionate argument. The second thing to note was that he'd included an excellent get-out clause for her. Most people had their Sundays planned by Friday evening.

'Sunday lunch?'

He shrugged. 'Yeah. Chicken probably, with roast potatoes and a few trimmings. Unless you're a vegetarian, in which case I'll think of something else...'

'I know what Sunday lunch is. I'm just not sure what I've done to earn the invitation.'

He shrugged. 'I reckon we have two options. Sit down somewhere neutral and get to know each other, or soundproof my office and wait for the next time. The first isn't quite as expensive or disruptive as the second.'

Or they could avoid each other completely. She was suddenly very grateful that John hadn't put that one on the table.

'Okay. I'd like to bring a dessert if that's okay. Just to show my commitment to the idea.'

'That's much appreciated. Maybe if we get to know each other a bit more, cut each other a bit of slack, then we can both apologise with a clear conscience.'

It was a good thought. They were trapped in a fascination with each other that wasn't going to go away, and making their peace wasn't just a good idea from a work point of view, it was something that Reba wanted. It seemed that John wanted it too.

'That would be nice, thank you for suggesting it. What time should I come?'

'Does any time between twelve and one suit you?'

'That's fine. I'll be there.'

John nodded. 'Thanks. I'll see you then.'

It was only after he'd got to his feet and was halfway back to the doors into the therapy room that it occurred to her.

'John. Where do you live?'

Reba thought she saw him smile in the darkness. They'd only met two weeks ago, but somehow it felt that they'd known each other for a long time, and she should already know where he lived.

'Eight Marvell Avenue. You turn left by the cinema on the High Street and then fourth right. Got your phone?'

Reba took her phone from her pocket and he rattled out his number. Then he turned, walking away.

This was practically a work lunch. There had been no need to spend fifteen minutes in the supermarket, sorting through the vegetables to find the best ones, and certainly no need to tidy up quite so thoroughly. Rosalie had decided to imitate his efforts and rearrange her toybox, and when the doorbell rang at exactly half past twelve, half its contents were still scattered across the floor.

His daughter crowded at his legs as he opened the door, jumping up and down with excitement. Reba was standing on the doorstep, looking wonderful in a boldly patterned wraparound skirt, secured at her waist with a wide leather belt, a black top and a thick knitted woollen jacket. She was always striking—her dark hair and strong features made sure of that. Beautiful—there was no doubt of that either. It occurred to John that she was probably the most interesting woman he'd ever met, and that seemed so much more than the sum of those parts.

'Come in.' Rosalie hadn't forgotten her manners, even if John was staring at her wordlessly. 'Everything's ready...'

So much for making this seem like a casual Sunday lunch. Reba ignored the suggestion, smiling and stepping into the hallway, bending down towards Rosalie.

'I brought something for us to eat.'

She held on to the glass bowl she was cradling, peeling back the silver paper that covered it. Rosalie leaned in, peering at the contents.

'Strawberries...!'

'You like strawberry trifle?'

Rosalie nodded. 'You have to give the food to Dad. You can give your coat to me.'

'Right you are.' Reba beamed at her, straightening up and thrusting the bowl into John's hands. Then she took her jacket off, handing it to Rosalie, who trailed it across the hall floor, climbing the bottom two stairs so that she could reach to hook it over the newel post.

He shot her an apologetic look, brushing a few specks of dust from the sleeve of her jacket as he made for the kitchen, and Reba laughed, telling him not to worry about that.

'Something smells nice...'

'It'll be ready in half an hour.' Opening the fridge to make space for the trifle, John pulled out a bottle. 'Would you like some wine?'

This all felt so strange. They weren't quite friends and yet they weren't enemies either. He'd known her for little more than two weeks, and yet he could almost see what Reba was thinking at times. It had all seemed so simple when he'd seen her sitting outside in the darkness—either continue on in an escalating round of arguments, or make their peace. He hadn't considered what a peace between him and Reba might look like.

She shook her head. 'I'm driving so I don't want too much. Maybe a glass at lunchtime.'

This was nerve-racking... And then Rosalie piped up. 'I'll show you the bathroom so you can wash your hands. It's next to *my* room.'

'Maybe later on, eh, Rosie...?' John fell silent as a lump formed in his throat, at the brilliance of Reba's sudden smile.

'That's very thoughtful of you, Rosalie. If it's okay...?' She flashed a querying look at John and he nodded. If Reba didn't mind, then Rosalie's decision to play the hostess was certainly taking the awkwardness out of the situation.

'This way.' Rosalie flounced out of the kitchen and Reba followed, turning to shoot him a smile as she went.

He could hear them upstairs. Rosalie had dropped another heavy hint that Reba might like to see her room, and the footsteps above his head and the sound of Rosalie's excited voice and Reba's laughter moved to the back of the house. If he'd stopped in his ever increasingly panicky trajectory and thought about it for a moment he might have realised that Rosalie would be an excellent partner in this enterprise. But then a five-year-old had a habit of going their own way, and John doubted he could have schooled Rosalie into doing anything better than this.

Maybe he should be *her* wingman. The lunch

was taking care of itself for ten minutes and he took two glasses from the cupboard, making a pretend cocktail for Rosalie with orange juice and fizzy lemonade, and adding a paper umbrella and a cherry. For Reba, half a glass of wine.

He found them in Rosalie's room, sitting on the two wicker chairs by the window. Rosalie's stance mimicked Reba's, her legs crossed and one elbow leaning on the arm of the chair, and they were clearly discussing the bird feeder that hung outside the window. Reba caught sight of him and gave him the smile that always made his knees go weak.

'Drinks! How lovely... Thank you.'

Rosalie beamed at him as John set the drinks down on the small table between them. 'Lunch is in ten minutes.'

This was important to Rosalie—having a room of her own, somewhere that she felt was hers and where she could bring her friends. He was grateful to Reba for her obvious appreciation of Rosalie's wish to play hostess.

He turned, hiding his smile. Rosalie didn't need him here, in the best possible way.

CHAPTER SEVEN

THE BEST WAY that Reba could describe lunch was that it was civil. That in itself was an achievement, since every instinct seemed to cry out that the very last thing she wanted to be with John was civil. That was the problem—it meant that even the slightest spark between them had the potential to explode into flames.

But Rosalie's presence precluded any flames this afternoon. The little girl had been so eager to welcome Reba and show her room off to her, and that had set the tone. Bringing drinks upstairs, to give it all the feel of a girls' get-together, had been a nice touch on John's part and after he'd gone back downstairs Rosalie had taken Reba's lead and sipped her pretend cocktail instead of drinking it down all at once.

And John made a mean roast, with all the trimmings. They rounded it off with the trifle, and then Rosalie, who'd reached her limit in terms of sitting still for one day, ran to the mess of toys that had been hastily pushed into a pile in the corner of the lounge area of the long open-plan ground floor. John fetched the coffee and showed Reba through a set of glass doors which led to a conservatory. He could keep an eye on Rosalie, who seemed intent on taking up as much floor space as possible to sort her toys into some kind of order, but when he closed the connecting doors they were alone.

Somehow, the temperature seemed to rise a couple of degrees. Probably not the conservatory's fault—the space was shaded by a couple of huge ferns at either end, and was very clearly a place for plants with some seating added as an afterthought. But whenever she was alone with John the room became warmer...

'Rosalie's room is lovely. And such nice colours.' Maybe if they *talked* about her then it would be a good second best to having her presence.

He nodded, seeming to relax back into his chair in the dappled green of the space. This was clearly John's quiet place in the house.

'That was thanks to Cathy. I was busy painting it pink and she came round and gave me a lecture on how little girls don't always prefer pink. She told me to choose a few colours that I reckoned we could live with for more than ten minutes, and let Rosalie pick the one she liked.'

Reba couldn't help smiling. 'The more I hear about Cathy, the more I really like her. You were friends before you took the job at the hospital?'

Maybe she shouldn't question him. John's way of dealing with things was not to talk about them, and today was supposed to be all about making their peace.

But he nodded. 'Yes, Cathy split her time between four different units, and when I was just qualified and working in the paediatric A&E department of my previous hospital I met her there. We had a lot of kids coming in with injuries after a school bus collided with a lorry and turned over onto its side. That was an awful day, and I was just starting to wonder how any of us were ever going to get through it when I found Cathy, sitting with a little boy whose arm was broken, holding him and singing to him.'

Reba nodded. 'That's a nice memory to have of her.'

John smiled suddenly. Not the arm's length smile that he used to ward off any hint of real feeling, but one that ran the gamut of emotions between sadness and fond remembrance.

'She was one of the best. When I adopted Rosalie I reckoned I knew what I needed to do to look after her, because I'd known her ever since she was a baby. I learned pretty quickly that there's a difference between being an involved uncle and a father. Cathy had two girls of her own who are grown-up now, and she came to my rescue with a lot of good advice.'

'It's good that you had someone like her.'

He nodded. 'Are you about to tell me that it's good to talk about that?'

Something hovered in the still air between them. The possibility of Reba rushing in and speaking her mind. Rosalie was on the other side of the glazed doors but she was in sight, and while her presence meant that there wouldn't be raised voices, there was still the possibility of a vehemently whispered disagreement that would result in Reba bidding him a tight-lipped good-bye and going home.

She didn't want to set foot on that path. She wanted to stay.

'I'm not about to tell you anything. I came here to listen.'

That smile again. The one that told her that John was slowly letting his guard down.

'Yeah. I asked you here with the intention of listening too.'

They sat in silence for a few moments. It was hard, being here with John and feeling all that she felt for him but wouldn't recognise, without having the comforting disguise of conflict to pour her emotions into. Reba reminded herself that it wasn't her style to shrink from a challenge.

'I really love Rosalie's room. I didn't have a room to myself when I was little.'

'You have brothers and sisters?'

She shook her head. 'No, but space wasn't the reason. We were always on the move, travelling with my father.'

'That sounds…different.' John seemed to be carefully avoiding making any value judgements, and Reba laughed. He was nothing if not true to his word.

'Most children think that normal is whatever *their* family does—I certainly did. It was a great way to grow up, we lived in so many beautiful cities and whichever house we were renting at the time was full of wonderful musicians whenever my parents threw a party. But I never had a room like Rosalie's, where I could keep all those things that kids keep. Name me one person you know who doesn't still have a pebble that they picked up when they were little, somewhere.'

He thought for a moment, and then got to his feet. 'You've got me wondering, now…'

John walked out into the main room, opening a drawer in the long, low sideboard in the dining area. Whatever he was looking for must be at the back and as he reached in Rosalie ran over to see what he was doing. They exchanged a few words then Rosalie raced away and Reba heard her thundering up the stairs.

She'd obviously started something. John clearly hadn't found what he was looking for here and he extended his search, moving to the kitchen. Reba followed him and found him emptying a drawer that seemed to be full of useful things—a light bulb, a screwdriver and several pieces of shaped plastic that didn't have any obvious use but must fit somewhere.

'Ah! Got it...' He grinned, reaching for the back of the drawer, and Reba held out her hand. His fingers brushed her palm as he dropped something cool into it.

'That's lovely.' A piece of dark blue sea glass, frosted over by the water.

'I'd forgotten I even had it.' John leaned in, turning it over in her hand as if this was the first time he'd seen it.

The ever-present heat rose suddenly. His scent seemed to fill her senses, together with a sudden longing to feel his touch again. When she looked up at him, his gaze seemed to devour her.

And then he stepped back. Sensible. She should have done that a lot sooner. John reached into the drawer again, and took out two more pieces of sea glass and a round pebble with a hole in it.

'I used to have quite a collection. I reckoned that sea glass must be very old for it to have frosted over like that, and I imagined a Viking sailor dropping it over the side of his boat...'

Reba smiled. 'Did the Vikings make glass?'

'No idea. Don't spoil it for me.'

A little piece of his child's imagination that she could hold in her hand. This seemed so special.

'If you hold the stone up you can actually look through the hole. I had an evolving set of theories about that...'

Reba would have liked to know what happened when you looked through the hole in the stone, but it seemed that piece of magic wasn't to be. Rosalie's footsteps sounded on the stairs and she pushed between them, clutching a plastic box to her chest.

'I've got more than Dad...'

But nothing quite so special. Reba closed her fingers around John's treasures, feeling the powerful spell they cast. Then she tipped them back into his hand, his fingers closing around hers a little as she did so.

One exchanged glance of regret that told her he felt it too. That little piece of his past that had become all-important for being shared. Then Reba smiled down at Rosalie, who had planted the box on the kitchen counter now. John lifted her up, sitting her next to it, and Rosalie took the lid from the box. Reba caught her breath, her wonder not quite as keen as the one she'd felt when John had found his small treasures.

'You *have* got a lot. Would you like to show me…?'

The afternoon that had promised to contain everything that John feared the most had become golden. Maybe not quite *easy* because John was still on edge, still wondering if this was wise on so many levels. Allowing someone in again, after he'd sealed himself off from the people around him, maintaining his usual face with the world while constantly on the run from the things that hurt. Allowing *Reba* in, someone who he hardly knew but so badly wanted to touch. That had been just as terrifying as he'd anticipated, but he hadn't reckoned on it feeling right and natural as well, in a world where lately everything had been feeling wrong.

'I don't want to keep you—but you're welcome to stay for tea…'

It had been raining all afternoon, but the time had flown. The house had become a playground, sorting through Rosalie's box of stones, selecting books from the shelves and recommending things to read to each other… Everything that Reba touched seemed to gain a piece of her magic. Even the small plants in the conservatory, that he and Rosalie were nursing along, seemed to straighten and stand to attention when Reba gave them a laughing pep talk about how much more growing they had left to do.

'It's still tipping it down. I will stay for tea if that's all right…?'

The non sequitur was clearly an excuse. Rain wasn't going to stop Reba from going out to her car and going home now, pressing ahead from each completed task with the smiling determination that he'd seen at the hospital. But she wanted to stay, and he wanted her to stay.

'Nothing to do for the morning?' The question just slipped out before he could stop it. Apparently that urge to throw a spanner into the works, and see how she reacted, was still there…

For a moment he thought she was going to rise to the implied challenge and that he'd messed everything up. Then suddenly she laughed. 'What do you think, John? I've always got something to do for tomorrow morning at work. But a woman has to eat.'

There were a thousand answers to that. John swallowed them down because they all had an element of the judgemental, and turned his attention to settling Rosalie down in front of the

TV with the favourite film she'd been clamouring to watch for the last ten minutes. Maybe Reba would sit down with her, when he walked back to the kitchen...

But he heard her footsteps behind him. She plumped herself down on the sofa at one end of the kitchen, shifting slightly to remove one of Rosalie's building bricks from the cushion and putting it onto the low table in front of her with the pile of other bricks.

'Sorry, they get everywhere.'

Reba shrugged, smiling. 'You're not going to ask...?'

'Ask what?' John decided that playing dumb was probably the more tactful option and Reba rolled her eyes.

'How much I have to do for tomorrow morning when I get home.'

John thought carefully about his answer. 'Today was meant to be all about not rising to the temptation of discussing what we each thought the other should be doing about their lives.'

'That's fair.' She leaned back into the sofa, crossing her legs.

'But you're still at liberty to tell me when I need to chase you away to get on with whatever it is you do have to do. I have a spare umbrella if keeping dry on the way to your car is a concern.' He looked out of the kitchen window. It had stopped raining now anyway, but the sky was still overcast and it could start again at any time.

Hearing Reba laugh seemed to satisfy his craving to prompt a reaction from her. 'I was up early this morning and I have everything I absolutely *need* to do for tomorrow finished.'

He was sure she could have found something else if she tried. John bit his tongue and nodded, reaching for the bread and a carving knife.

'I'm currently struggling with the things I don't need to do.' Reba supplied the answer, as if she knew that was going to be his next question. 'It's my hothouse mentality.'

Now she'd lost him completely. John felt that the comment begged his question. 'Hothouse? You want to revisit the conservatory?'

She laughed. 'Not *your* conservatory, no. I grew up in a different kind of hothouse, where music was everything. There was always more practice, always more to be achieved.'

'You didn't want that?' It was a new concept for John. Reba always seemed to take such joy from her music.

'I wanted it. I started learning the piano when I was four, and the violin when I was five. Our house always had musicians coming and going, and my favourite thing was being allowed to play with them.'

'Did you ever think of performing as a career?'

'At one point that was the only thing I thought about. I changed my mind, though. What would you say is the most important? Performing to a packed auditorium of people, or using music to heal sick kids?'

He laid down the carving knife, reckoning that was enough bread for sandwiches. 'Trick question. What do you expect me to say? Although I imagine that a lot of good things come out of performing to an auditorium as well.'

'Yes, that's good too. But I decided to go with the sick kids. When I finished my degree in music I pretended to do the rounds of auditions and performances, but instead I was taking an MA in Music Therapy. When Hans—my father—found out he was incandescent.'

'He didn't know?'

'He and my mother were in South America— he was playing a season of concerts there. My parents phoned me every week and asked me how I was doing, and I said *great* and that I was working hard. By the time they got back to London it was all a done deal, I'd already lost six months of knocking on every door in town looking for performance opportunities and was halfway through my MA. It was all a disaster of epic proportions in his eyes.'

'You're giving me chills. Is this what Rosalie and I have to look forward to?'

Reba chuckled. 'I very much doubt it. The trick is to ask her what she wants, instead of just assuming. And allowing her to say anything in reply, without exploding.'

'I'll bear that in mind.' Maybe it was a way forward with Reba as well. No assuming and no exploding. 'I take it that your father did explode?'

'That wasn't such a big thing as it sounds. He's volatile at the best of times, and sometimes that's wonderful, but he has a habit of throwing things when he can't cope with his emotions.'

'Things that break?' John remembered the balled-up paper that Reba had thrown and realised the gesture was a little more than just the delightful expression of emotion that he'd taken it for.

'The more breakable the better. When it became impossible to hide the fact that I'd decided on a change of career, he was furious. He said that I was wasting all the opportunities I'd had, and he was never going to forgive me. It was a good six months before he'd even speak to me again.'

John wasn't sure what to say. Reba had described it as if it were almost a joke, but he saw real hurt in her face. She was sitting bolt upright now, as if still needing to defend herself. He forgot about the sandwiches, turning to lean against the kitchen counter, facing her.

'We got over it. Hans makes sure to throw a few comments about me wasting my talent whenever he sees me and I ask him when he last helped a child to recover from life-changing injuries. My mother generally gets in between us and...' Reba shrugged. 'I guess we love each other, even if we don't agree.'

And Reba had something to prove. Her dogged determination to be the best, making leaflets and staging concerts, wasn't just because she was committed to her work. She was driven by her childhood and her father's clear message that she'd settled for second best, which dismissed everything that she was achieving now.

'When I first adopted Rosalie I had to learn how to stop being a favourite uncle, and start being a dad. Less of a friend, and more someone who'd always be there for her and accept her.' He shrugged. Maybe that wasn't relevant.

'That's exactly it. Hans gave me a wonderful childhood. He was my mentor and my friend. Somehow he seemed to lose the *dad* part.'

'But you didn't.'

'Does any child? His disappointment in me really hurt.'

'So what made you change your mind about your career?'

'I was part of a quartet that played in schools and homes for the elderly. Hospitals…anywhere that would have us, really. We started off thinking that this was a way to perform together in lots of different environments, and then suddenly the environment became a great deal more important to me than the performing. I talked to a therapist at one of the hospitals we visited and… I just knew that this was what I wanted to do.'

He nodded. 'I can identify with that. When I went to medical school, I had ideas of being at the cutting-edge of my chosen field, whatever that turned out to be. It wasn't until I rotated onto Paediatrics that I realised that the cutting-edge that I wanted to be on was a child's smile. It's all just a matter of priorities.'

Reba gave him a delicious grin. 'You'd be surprised how many people will tell me differently when they find out I had the opportunity to play professionally…'

She fell silent suddenly, listening. Rosalie was singing along to her film, and John imagined that she was also replicating the actions.

'She does that a lot—' He fell silent as Reba

pressed her fingers across her lips in an urgent message to be quiet. She got to her feet, walking quietly to the kitchen door to listen. John couldn't resist joining her, wondering what had caught Reba's attention.

'Did you hear that?' She smiled up at him.

'She really likes the song.'

'And she hit every single note.' Reba was whispering vehemently, as if she were in a concert hall and someone was about to shush *her*.

'Yes, she does. When I try to sing along with her, she puts her hand over my mouth. She tells me that I don't do it right.' John was beginning to catch Reba's meaning and the familiar tension curled in his stomach. All the things that he might need to do to make Rosalie happy. All the mistakes that he could make...

'Are you telling me that Rosalie's musically gifted?'

'I'm saying that she has a good ear. She can hit a note and she can tell when you don't.' Reba looked up at him in surprise. 'Is that a problem?'

Maybe. John didn't know and that was what was killing him at the moment. He turned away from her, ignoring the half-made sandwiches and going to sit down on the sofa. He had to think about this.

Reba came to sit next to him. The temptation

to reach for her, tell her that he wasn't sure how to keep Rosalie safe from all of the gazillion things that might be a problem and might not...

It was almost a surprise to find that he *hadn't* reached for her. It had seemed so clear in his mind that he could hardly tell the difference between that and the stunned silence that he'd maintained.

'John. Is it a problem?'

He could ask. Reba was a professional musician and it was natural to seek her opinion. That couldn't be construed as seeking comfort.

'I don't know... What do you do with a child who has a good ear?' Let alone one who was musically gifted—that was a scale of challenge he didn't dare contemplate.

She reached out, brushing the back of his hand with her fingers. Even that small contact made him shiver and she pulled her arm back as if she'd been stung, turning the corners of her mouth down.

'Look, I wouldn't presume to tell anyone how to raise their child. I'd find it terrifying to have that little life in my hands. But this I know about. Rosalie seems to have a good ear for music, and if that's the case then it might— just might—bring her as much joy as it has me over the years. That's all you need to know right now. My own experience tells me that if she wants to play you won't need to push her. Just don't have any expectations.'

Reba was speaking from the heart. Her passion showed through, but that just touched a place in his own heart, which allowed him to reach out a little.

'So what would you advise? Practically speaking.'

'Let her listen to music—local parks often do great concerts, which are good for kids because they're informal and she can stay as long as she likes, or go and do something else. Maybe put an instrument in her hand and see what she does with it. I have a glockenspiel at home that she can try. It has a nice tone.'

John couldn't help laughing. 'You make that sound as if it's every little girl's dream.'

'Some kids like dolls or train sets. I was pretty fond of the glockenspiel, until the piano took its place.' Reba gave a shrugging grin. 'I imagine there was a lot that was hard about adopting Rosalie. This isn't hard at all.'

It was an invitation to talk. One that John had extended to Reba but he now realised that it was a lot easier to listen than to talk. One day, maybe, he'd tell her about the tearing fears that could still leave him almost breathless.

'Thanks. And if Rosie could try your glockenspiel out I'd be very grateful. It sounds like a
fun thing to do...'

CHAPTER EIGHT

REBA HAD STAYED at John's house for longer than she'd meant to. Rosalie's energy had started to flag suddenly, and she'd gone to her dad, getting up onto his lap. She'd followed the conversation for a while and then her eyelids began to droop.

'I'd better be getting her to bed.'

'Yes!' Reba shot to her feet. She'd got too comfortable here, and she did have a few things to be getting on with at home. 'I should be making a move.'

John left Rosalie curled up on the sofa, and walked with her into the hallway to see her out. This lone goodbye presented yet another challenge——to kiss or not to kiss? Reba decided to act as she would with any other friend, and stood on her toes to brush a kiss against his cheek.

She felt the light touch of his fingers on her shoulder, his hand suddenly snatched away. All the same it was all kinds of wonderful to be this close to him. As she stepped back, she realised that she was still holding on to his arm, and felt herself redden.

'I guess that needs a bit of work.' He smiled suddenly and everything seemed all right again.

'I reckon so. Thank you for a lovely afternoon, I really enjoyed myself.'

'My pleasure.' His hand found hers, his fingers cool against her skin. A moment of slight pressure that told her he really meant what he'd said, and then he stepped away, opening the door for her.

And then she was outside in the cool evening air, making for her car. Feeling relief, because she *hadn't* done what she'd really wanted to do and kissed John's mouth. And he hadn't done what she'd really wanted him to do and responded. Because the only passion that she had room for in her life was music and the career that she was making for herself.

Driven to make for herself, in pursuit of Hans' forgiveness and his approval. In those quiet moments of conversation she'd seen that in a different light. She shrugged the thought off, getting into her car.

So much for good intentions. They'd lasted for nearly two days, although admittedly for one of those days Reba had been working with private patients and hadn't been anywhere near the hospital. If you counted it in terms of time spent within hailing distance of each other it came to around eight hours.

Reba had bumped into him on her way into work on Tuesday, and they'd exchanged a smiling hello. Then she'd retreated to the therapy room, and a full schedule of appointments with her patients.

The first note had been clipped to the front of one of the patient files.

Looking forward to seeing how Meera's sessions go. Please let me know.

The second was waiting for her in her pigeon-hole at lunchtime.

The rounders team is a person down. Interested?

The third had been sent via Joanne, who happened to be passing. Reba unfolded the sheet of paper and glanced at it. Apparently John had a sudden urge to know about current research on how music therapy could help autistic children. This one was signed with a single 'J' and that small intimacy made her shiver.

'Is Dr Thornton's email not working?'

Joanne shrugged. 'I should be so lucky. He's been emailing me about one thing or another all day.'

So John was clearly in a mood to say something, and Reba guessed it had very little to do with what was contained in his various notes. There was only one way to find out.

She had to wait because she had two more patients to see, but at five-thirty she made her way up to John's office. There was no need to knock, the door was wide open and he had obviously just returned from the wards, his sleeves rolled up from scrubbing his hands.

'Reba...' He turned, giving her that melting look that turned her legs to jelly. Reba reminded herself that jelly wouldn't get her anywhere in this situation. If her friendship with John was based on anything, it was based on honesty.

'I've got some answers for you...' She approached his desk and he perched himself on the near side of it, apparently unwilling to give her the advantage of something solid between them. Fair enough. Hand to hand combat, up close and personal.

'First...' She laid his first note on the desk. 'Yes, I'm looking forward to seeing how music therapy might help Meera. It's not always successful in helping with asthma, but if someone enjoys singing and making music then it may give specific benefits. I'll keep you informed.'

'Great. Thank you.'

She'd wanted to see that smile. The real smile that he didn't take a moment to think about before he put it into effect. *Careful what you wish for, Reba,* because now it was playing havoc with her sense of purpose.

'Second… No, thanks, I'll give it a miss.'

'Really?' He raised an eyebrow. 'Your loss, the rounders matches are good fun.'

'Are you speaking from experience or is that just what you've heard?' Reba smiled sweetly at him.

'It's what I've heard. I was thinking it was about time I started supporting the team.'

'It probably is, but you're on your own with that. I don't do that kind of thing—smashed fingers or a sprained wrist could be a real problem for me.' She held up her hand, silencing him as he opened his mouth to speak. 'And before you say that I could be an idle spectator, remember who you're speaking with.'

'Good point. You *never* watch sports, then?'

'I don't watch. I might cheerlead, or organise the refreshments or even do a bit of coaching…' Reba smiled at him. 'Only you probably don't want to be on the other end of my coaching demands.'

'I'll bear that in mind.' He leaned forward, taking the second slip of paper from her grasp and putting it onto his desk. 'Next?'

'No answer. If you want to know about current research then do what everyone else does, and send me an email. I'll return it promptly with helpful links.'

He took the final piece of paper from her hand, screwing it up into a tight ball and throwing it in the direction of the wastepaper bin. It hit the wall and dropped onto the floor.

'You missed.' Suddenly her gaze was locked with his, and Reba's heart began to beat faster. *Don't... Don't be excited by every little thing that contains some hint of passion.*

'Yeah. Not quite so satisfying when you don't hit the mark.'

'I wouldn't know. I always manage to hit the mark...' She grinned up at him. 'It's a matter of practice. I've never played rounders, but I've coached.'

A slow smile spread across his face. 'Yeah? I expect you could show me just how it's done, then.'

Oh, yes. She wanted to show him exactly how it was done. 'It's all in the balance. And the rhythm, of course.'

He nodded. 'I reckoned that rhythm would come into it somewhere. Any chance of a demonstration?'

Reba took a step closer, taking hold of his wrist. 'It's better if you stand up...'

He got to his feet, his bulk towering over her.

Reba tried not to catch her breath. 'You have to get the angle just right...'

She manoeuvred his arm back, then started to move it slowly through a throwing arc. The higher his arm went, the closer she was drawn in, stretching to reach his wrist. She found herself pressing against him and when she tried to step back his other hand coiled around her waist.

'We should stop, John...' She felt him let go of her suddenly, stepping back. 'I meant... *I* should stop. Because...' Reba gestured over her shoulder at the half open door.

He nodded, grinning suddenly. 'You could always shut it. If you wanted.'

She walked back to the door, swinging it closed. When she turned, John was watching her thoughtfully. 'Now what? We argue?'

Suddenly, Reba knew what she wanted. With the kind of absolute clarity that only seemed to hit after a whole succession of mistakes. 'I don't want to argue with you, John.'

She could see it in his eyes. He wanted exactly the same as she did, but they were both afraid to ask. Both far too wary of tipping their lives upside down. Since when had Reba been afraid of rash gestures and bold moves?

Ever since she had something to lose. Since she'd learned to pile all of her passion into ambition, and showing everyone that she was the best at what she did. Waiting…always waiting for Hans to recognise that.

She took a step towards him, laying her shaking fingers on his chest. Feeling his heart beat faster. John had a lot to lose too, the carefully constructed life that meant he could look after Rosalie and continue to steer the department into excellence. The life that was going to crumble if he didn't stop and give his own emotions a chance to make themselves heard.

'What *do* you want, Reba?'

Each one of her movements seemed mirrored in his. When she slowly reached up to lay her hand on the back of his collar she felt his arm circle her waist, barely touching her. As she stretched up, he bent his head. Lost in his gaze and the exquisite anticipation of the moments that seemed inevitable now, she brushed a kiss against his cheek.

The increasing pressure of his hand on her back allowed her to move closer. She spread her fingers across the back of his head, and suddenly he was kissing her. The passion that they'd both denied, because it was inconvenient in their lives, spilled over suddenly…

So much from one kiss. Passion, rage and vulnerability. Arousal that escalated out of control until it seemed that they were passing a point of no return. John held her close, his fingers exploring the sensitive skin behind her ear and moving further to tangle in her hair.

Then suddenly he moved back. Holding her, his fingers tender against the skin of her cheek.

'Not here...'

'Not ever?' Reba felt her lower lip quiver at the thought.

'I didn't say that...'

A knock sounded at the door. They had about two seconds to compose themselves before whoever it was would be on their way in, and Reba had just lost those seconds thinking about it. John had moved faster, and put three feet of empty space between them.

'Oh, sorry...' Joanne looked startled. 'Didn't realise you were in conference.'

'That's okay, Joanne, we were just about finished...' Thankfully John had decided not to look at her while he delivered the barefaced denial.

'It's just a quick question. I can come back.' Joanne turned to leave but John beckoned her into the office.

'Ask me now. You'll be downstairs, Reba?'

'Yes, I...think I left the leaflets you wanted in my car...' Oddly, her voice sounded relatively normal and her brain was functioning again, telling her that she and John needed to get away from the hospital and find some neutral ground somewhere.

'I'll see you there, then. Just for once, let's all get out of here at five-thirty...'

There was just one thing that John needed to say to Reba and then he would let things take their course, expecting nothing. All of his senses, every last instinct, wanted all that their kiss had promised and tonight he wasn't sure he could bear to let her go. But the one thing he knew for sure was that Reba had to be the one to make that decision.

'Rosalie's with my parents tonight.' There. He'd done it and Reba could make whatever she wanted of the information.

'My place, then?' She looked up at him, her hair glinting in the sunlight. 'Unless you have to be at home.'

'I have my phone.' All they needed were these blunt practicalities. Everything else was already there, all of the passion and all of the answers to his questions, flashing in her eyes.

Reba got into her car, winding down the window to tell him the address and ask if he knew how to get there.

'I'll follow you.' Wherever she went. Wherever *this* went. Despite all of his fears, and the sure knowledge that the kind of letting-go that he experienced with Reba could shake loose the anchors that kept his life on track.

But the fifteen minutes alone in his car couldn't make him change his mind. He and Reba were something he'd never encountered before, a relationship that just wouldn't stay where they'd both decided to put it. One that pushed way past his boundaries and yet still left him smiling to himself when no one was looking.

Her house was at the end of a quiet cul-de-sac, which led down to a footpath with a small urban waterway on the other side. The purple front door led into a narrow hallway, the afternoon sun slanting through the open door of the sitting room. John had thought a lot about what Reba's home might be like, but now he didn't even glance at his surroundings because she'd slammed the front door shut and taken him into her arms.

'You can't fix me. You know that...?' This didn't *feel* like one of Reba's projects, it was too uncertain and had far too many loose ends to it. But he still had to ask.

'I know. I'll take you just as you are.' Reba kissed him and a sheer, brilliant feeling exploded deep in his chest.

'With nothing more to offer you than just this?'

'This is what I want, John. You can't fix me either, and I have a lot of things to do and places to be.'

'Not tonight, though.' He turned her round, backing her against the wall. When she flung her arms around his neck he lifted her, feeling their bodies lock together as she wrapped her legs around his hips.

'Not tonight...' Her dark eyes became even darker as he unzipped her jacket with an assertive confidence that surprised even him. Reba was clinging to him, her cheeks flushed and her lips parted, ready to welcome his kiss.

They'd gone from nought to a hundred in seconds flat, and he could hardly think straight. Then everything else fell away as he slipped his hand inside her jacket, feeling the heat of her body beneath the soft cotton of her shirt. He belonged to Reba now, and the only thing he had to do was to try and deserve that.

He kissed her and sheer happiness flooded through him. He knew they'd be lying down together before too long, but he wanted this to last just a little longer. And then his world tipped again as Reba nuzzled against his neck, whispering just two words into his ear.

'Upstairs. Now.'

CHAPTER NINE

REBA HAD THROWN the duvet hastily across the bed this morning, dressed in a hurry and not looked back before hurrying downstairs to grab toast and coffee. If she'd known, she would have tidied up a bit.

But there was no stopping this swelling tide of passion and Reba reckoned that John wasn't going to be inspecting for dust. She wriggled free of his embrace, hustling him up the stairs and into her bedroom.

The first time with anyone was always a matter of negotiation. And in the grip of this maelstrom of desire they tested each other. John's determination, his passion against hers. Her wins, when she found herself owning the moment and he gave himself up to her. Her delicious losses, when she lost all sense of time and space and felt only his caress.

'Condoms?' Even that slice of practicality held a promise that made her shiver.

'Top drawer of the dresser…' Reba changed her mind about letting him find them and broke free of him, opening and closing the drawer quickly so he couldn't see the jumbled contents. As he reached to take the condoms from her she snatched them away, hiding them behind her back.

'What would you have done if I hadn't had any?'

'Maybe I would have left you here and run all the way to the nearest chemist.' He grinned when he saw her look of dismay at the thought. 'Or maybe resorted to creative improvisation.'

The feel of his lips against her neck, his hand on hers as he teased the packet from her fingers, left Reba in no doubt that his backup plan would have been wonderful too. 'There are only three in the packet.'

'Then we can find out what happens when we have to make do without.' He must have felt her shiver at the thought, because his voice took on a teasing note. 'Later…'

The smart answer wasn't going to wash. Three weren't going to be enough to quell the desire that was raging through her, filling her mind as well as her body. John was all action now, tossing the condoms onto the pillow and picking her up, laying her down on top of the rumpled duvet. When she reached to pull him down with her onto the bed he batted her hands away, bending to unzip her ankle boots and strip off her socks, tossing them onto the floor.

His shirt was already half undone, and he pulled it over his head. Marvellous. Reba could imagine her fingers playing a melody of desire across those taut muscles. John's grey-blue eyes taunted her as he took off the rest of his clothes, and then moved quickly on to hers.

And still he teased her. He put off that moment when his skin touched hers in an embrace, shifting her round and smoothing her hair out on the pillows. Kissing her, and murmuring how much he wanted her. Reba reached for the condoms and suddenly the balance between them tipped again. He was all hers...

She didn't waste these moments, because they were precious and she knew they wouldn't last for long. Pulling him down, feeling his weight on her and the touch of his skin. Feeling his reaction as she guided him, almost losing her mind as he hooked one hand beneath her knee and moved deeper inside her.

Reba didn't need to beg him not to wait— there was no way either of them could stop this now. They moved together and cried out together. When she miscalculated, pushing him too far and too soon into a shuddering climax, he somehow managed to keep hold of his senses long enough for his fingers to coax her own orgasm from her trembling body.

'That was…only slightly short of perfect.' John shot her an apologetic look and Reba kissed away his frown.

'Did I give you any choice on the timing?'

He chuckled quietly. 'Not that I'm aware of. Are you okay?'

'It *was* perfect, John. I loved every moment of it.' She nestled against him, whispering into his ear. *'Especially the last part.'*

That seemed to reassure him, and he pulled her close into his embrace. 'I'll remember my manners next time. Ladies first…'

John had wanted so badly to be inside her when she reached her climax, but it seemed he'd have to wait for that experience. It was a complete mystery to him how he'd managed to keep from falling exhausted on the bed for long enough to make sure that she came too.

He couldn't promise her that it wouldn't happen again, just as he could never predict the outcome of any of the things that seemed to explode without warning between them. But this was the epicentre of it all, the place they'd feared going but which everything else had relentlessly mimicked. The way her music seemed to ooze passion. The arguments. John's insatiable curiosity about everything in her life, and their shared drive to fix each other. It had all been about this.

She'd started to shift against him as if she had something on her mind, and John opened one eye. 'You're thinking of throwing something?'

'No.' Reba kissed his cheek. 'I could do, if that's what floats your boat…'

'Nah. You floated my boat far better, just now.' He felt as if he were floating still. Bathed in the warm light of the evening, and bereft of all the things that seemed to weigh him down.

Reba chuckled. 'We'll keep the throwing things for those times when this isn't possible then. I was just wishing I'd tidied up a bit this morning.'

John looked around the bedroom, seeing it for the first time. An assortment of diverse pieces of furniture that seemed to go together so much better than if they'd matched. Walls and fabrics were cream, providing a backdrop for a set of framed line drawings on the wall, which looked as if they were originals rather than prints, and an eclectic mix of ceramics that lined the deep windowsill.

'If you have the urge to tidy up, then put your clothes on and we'll go over to my place.'

She laughed. 'You have a five-year-old to contend with.'

'Rosalie appears to have a natural sense of order. Which isn't always quite the same as tidy.' John kept everything tidy, but there was a deep disorder about it all that always gave him the feeling of chaos. This room had a continuity of feeling about it that would make sense even if everything wasn't necessarily in its right place.

'And you?'

'I just put everything where it's supposed to be, so I know where to find things. This room's nicer than that.'

He meant the observation as a compliment and Reba took it as one, smiling and snuggling against him. 'In that case, I think I'll just stay here.'

'I'm puzzled, though.' John looked around the room again. 'I thought you'd have at least one musical instrument in each room...'

'The back bedroom's my music room, they're all in there. Apart from the piano, that would have been very tricky to get upstairs. And a piano's more a living room kind of thing, don't you think?'

John had never really thought about it. 'See. Natural sense of order. What does that tell you about what we should do next?'

'I could take a shower... You could join me if you like. I'll show you my piano, and then make something to eat.' Reba seemed to be thinking of things in order of importance, and it was gratifying that she'd put showering with him ahead of the piano.

'No work to do…?' He'd been hoping that wouldn't feature in her to-do suggestions and made an insincere effort to make the comment sound like a joke.

'There's always work to do. Just not tonight.'

John couldn't help smirking in triumph at the thought that he'd managed to knock that entirely off the list. He must be doing something right.

'Then perhaps we should stay here a little longer before taking that shower. Just in case we're not quite done yet.'

She smiled, running her fingers across his chest. That warm, tingling feeling in the pit of his stomach and the way that she moved against him when his hand caressed her hip told him that they definitely weren't done with each other yet.

'Yes. It would be a pity to go to the trouble of putting our clothes back on, just to find we had to take them off again…'

They still weren't done with each other at ten o'clock, although it wouldn't have been humanly possible to act on that any further. John had succeeded in his resolution to show Reba he could hold out until she'd taken every moment of pleasure that she could, before he was shaken to the core by his own reaction. They'd slept a little and woken up hungry.

Watching her tie up her hair and walk naked to the bathroom was a whole new exercise in pleasure. Showering, dressing, walking downstairs even. Whatever she did fascinated him and he followed her in a kind of happy daze.

'Come and see my piano…' She almost danced into the sitting room and John felt himself running his hand across his creased shirt, as if he was about to be introduced to a member of the family.

The long room that stretched from the front of the house to the back was in much the same style as Reba's bedroom. An eclectic mix of furniture and fabrics which matched perfectly even though they shouldn't, set against plain cream walls. Everything seemed to be arranged around a gleaming upright piano, which seemed slightly deeper than others he'd seen and stood against the wall in the middle of the room, with the sitting area to one side of it and a dining table to the other.

Reba sat down on the long leather stool, beckoning for him to join her. 'It's the piano that my father used to take with him for practice when we travelled. It has a really good tone.'

The instrument oozed a quiet quality, and when Reba played a few notes the sound belied its size.

'He doesn't use it now?'

'No, now that he's a big star he has it written into his contract that he's provided with a grand, on loan, when he travels. This is the piano I learned on, and he gave it to me.'

'It's a lovely thing…' John hesitantly reached out to touch the keys and Reba nodded him on. A note sounded, pure and clear in the quiet of the night.

'I'm lucky to have it. It's not something I could afford all that easily.' She started to play, a simple melody that John recognised without knowing the name of it, which seemed to reach straight into his heart.

'What's that?' He almost choked on the words.

'Clair de Lune, by Claude Debussy. You like it?'

He nodded. John had revelled in the feeling that he was floating earlier, but the weight that usually burdened his heart did have one advantage, in not allowing him to feel all that much. He was defenceless now, and the music brought tears to his eyes.

This wasn't the time. John steeled himself against the loss that the music seemed to represent, turning on the seat to look away from the piano. Reba seemed to sense that something was wrong, and stopped playing suddenly.

'Sorry, Claude.' She seemed to be addressing the empty air. 'I'm just not feeling it at the moment.'

She started playing again and this time he recognised the piece. A waltz by Shostakovich, that seemed to encompass all of the romance of the dance. Eroticism even, but maybe that was just the way that Reba chose to play it. The thought made him smile, this new emotion more welcome than the last.

'Food.' Reba ended the piece with a dramatic chord. 'I don't have much in the fridge at the moment, but I do a mean toasted cheese sandwich. Or will the cheese make you dream?'

He nudged her shoulder with his, chuckling. 'It would be a waste of tonight not to dream.'

Reba laughed, getting up from the piano stool, her light step seeming to reproduce the airy precision of a waltz. She didn't just play, the music ran through her like an ever-changing tide.

Maybe he was getting himself into something that he shouldn't. But John had no choice, he was already mesmerised by her. He was just going to have to learn to handle it.

Reba had set her alarm for six, which would give John the chance to get home and then into work on time. She'd woken in his arms at five, and they'd welcomed in the dawn together before John dressed and went downstairs, grabbing his car keys as Reba handed him a cup of coffee.

'Have a great day.' He kissed her, seeming suddenly more distant. Hurrying away maybe, from something that he'd decided couldn't happen again. Reba had had her share of short-lived romances, which had drifted into oblivion as a succession of partners had realised that her music and her career pushed them into third place on her list of priorities. But she'd never had a one-night stand before, and she wasn't sure how to behave. Wasn't sure how to even ask if this really *was* a one-night stand.

She'd never had sex like this before either. And this was something that she wanted to keep.

'You too.' She took the cup from his hand, sipping the coffee. As if that could keep him here for a moment longer. 'I guess…maybe we can manage not to argue when we see each other again at work?'

His eyes softened suddenly. 'Last night wasn't a mediation exercise. Not for me, anyway. It was something that I wanted very much, and loved every moment of.'

Good… Good. Maybe she could ask…

'I loved it too, John.'

He nodded, taking his coffee back. They were standing in the hall, staring at each other like a couple of awkward teenagers who hadn't yet learned how to ask whether a parting was a *goodbye* or a *see you later*. Last night, desire had seemed a wonderful and all-encompassing thing, but this morning it was confusing.

'I want to ask… But I don't want to make this all about when I'm free, that's not fair to you.'

Reba caught her breath. John felt the same way she did, and his hesitancy was a matter of respect, not taking it for granted that she'd be able to fit in with his responsibilities, or that she'd even want to.

'Ask. Please ask.'

He smiled. 'My parents have taken Rosalie on a mid-week break in the Lake District, and they'll be back on Friday. I don't suppose you have tonight or tomorrow evening free?'

'I have a private client tonight, but I'm free on Thursday.'

'Yeah?' He smiled suddenly. 'If you'd like to come to my place, I can cook for you.'

'That would be nice, thank you. We can pretend it's not all about amazing sex...' Reba pressed her lips together. That hadn't been quite what she'd meant to say. 'I didn't mean to imply that last night was all about the sex.'

'I know. It wasn't for me either.' He put his coffee and keys down on the stairs, and took her in his arms. 'Although the sex was...*really* amazing.'

She could let him go now. They knew where they stood, even if it wasn't particularly easy ground for either of them. If they just kept talking, they could work it out.

CHAPTER TEN

REBA HAD MISSED JOHN. An ever-present thrill of longing had permeated the last two days, and she'd been less focused on her work. But no one had seemed to notice, and so far the sky hadn't fallen in on her head.

Maybe she'd be able to concentrate a little better when this wasn't all so new. And Reba had to admit that there had been a different joy in her sessions with her young clients. Not just in the music, although that remained, but in life itself.

John's front door opened before she got the chance to ring the bell. He was grinning, his phone held to his ear, and Reba walked quietly inside, putting her bag down in the hallway.

'No, sweetheart. Just because I'm having pizza tonight, it doesn't make it Pizza Night. It's not Pizza Night unless you're here.' Clearly he was talking to Rosalie.

'Okay. No, I won't enjoy it as much without

you.' He flashed Reba a grin, beckoning her into the kitchen.

'Yes… I'm glad you had a nice day with Gramps and Grandma. Sleep tight and I'll see you tomorrow. Does Grandma want to talk to me…?' John raised his eyebrows, looked at the phone and then put it down on the kitchen counter.

'Rosalie hung up on you?'

'Yes, she'd said all she wanted to say. I dare say my mother will call back if she wants to tell me anything.' John reached for her, curling his arms around her shoulders. 'But how was *your* day?'

His kiss still had the same hunger that had shaken her world two days ago. But now they had the confidence of knowing that whatever came next didn't have to be crammed into the space of one night, for fear that otherwise it might be lost for ever.

'Getting better by the minute. Although I'm disappointed that we won't be having Pizza Night.' The two pizzas that lay half-finished on the counter looked nice.

'We're at liberty to have pizza. We just can't call it Pizza Night, but since I won't be arranging the toppings into smiley faces, I think the distinction's clear enough.'

'No smiley faces? I'm devastated.'

'You're welcome to come on Pizza Night.' He pressed his lips together in a frown. 'Although—'

Reba laid her finger across his lips. 'I know. No staying the night when Rosalie's here. That's okay.'

'Is it? I don't want to confuse Rosalie, not right now when she's just starting to settle again. But the more I think about it, the less fair it seems to you.'

'It's not fair to me if I become someone who's going to unsettle your daughter, John. I knew exactly what I was getting into, right from the start. And I've got my own things to do, you know.'

'You mean cutting a swathe of excellence in your chosen profession?'

'Yes, as it happens. I thought we weren't going to try to fix each other.'

He laughed, bending to kiss her. 'You're quite right. And I don't need to fix you, you're perfect as you are.'

'Don't give me the task of being perfect, John, it's too much for either of us to aspire to. Just take me for who I am.' She returned his kiss, making this one last longer than the first.

'I'll take as much as you want to give. All I have to give you in return is pizza.'

And a raging heart. The storm of feeling behind John's controlled façade, which both excited her and made her sad because he didn't express those feelings often enough. But she'd made a promise, and fixing him wasn't an option.

'I'll take pizza. For now...'

Pizza and a glass of wine. They sat in the leafy conservatory as the sky darkened, talking and touching. Kissing. Happy to let the anticipation build, until they couldn't bear it any longer and thundered up the stairs. Hit again by the lightning of John's passion, and watching as he was hit by hers, until finally they curled up together to sleep.

But when Reba woke in the night he wasn't there. She rolled into the warmth of his side of the bed, expecting that he'd got up for some reason and would be back again soon. But as she lay awake the bed grew cooler, leaving her shivering and alone.

The house was quiet and she got out of bed, pulling the emerald-green wrap she'd brought with her across her shoulders and tying it at the waist. The bathroom door was ajar, and he wasn't there. When she padded quietly down the stairs, the kitchen and sitting room were both in darkness, but she saw a figure sitting in the shadows of the conservatory.

'John...?' He seemed to be lost in thought, and jumped when she spoke.

'Uh... Sorry, did I wake you?'

'No.' Reba hesitated in the doorway, wondering if he wanted to be alone. 'You want some company?'

His lips formed a smile in the darkness. One of those smiles that he had to think about first... Something was wrong, and perhaps he'd decided that he didn't want to talk about it.

'Sure.'

It wasn't exactly an invitation, but she decided to make it one. When she sat down next to him on the large wicker sofa he didn't reach to touch her.

'What's up?'

Silence. That was okay, she could just keep him company. Reba leaned back into the cushions, tucking her legs up underneath her in a signal that she wasn't going anywhere.

'I...don't know if I can do this, Reba. I thought I could, but...it's just not fair on you.'

What? They'd discussed this, hadn't they? Maybe there was something more that he hadn't told her yet. The dead look in his eyes told her that this wasn't simple practicalities. Reba took a breath. Her first impulse was to demand to know what was going on, but that was spurred by the sinking feeling that John might be about to end their relationship before it had even started. If she wanted to fight him on that, she had to take a gentler approach.

'Didn't I already tell you? It suits me as well.'

He turned to look at her, and she saw regret in his face as he shook his head.

'John, you're frightening me.' Terror was more the word. Reba swallowed it down. 'If there's something else, please tell me.'

Something registered. 'I never want to frighten you, Reba. I don't mean to.'

'I'll reword it, then. *I'm frightened because I think I'm about to lose you.* That's how I feel and I have a right to it. It's not your responsibility.' She heard annoyance creep into her tone, and bit it back.

Too late. John had heard it too and the ghost of a real smile showed in his face. Maybe battling him was the right way to go.

'Okay. Point taken. Maybe you are about to lose me, but that's my fault not yours.'

'John! I've had it with tiptoeing around you, just spit it out. Because this hurts...'

This was what he understood. He knew all about passion, and he knew about hurt too.

'I can't let it go, Reba. I feel something with you, and that makes me afraid. As if everything's going to come crashing down around me. I can't let that happen, but I can't shut you out either.'

Reba thought for a moment. 'Is this about your sister's death? And Cathy's?'

She thought she saw tears in his eyes. Her instinct was to shy away from that, to do something to change his mood, but that wasn't going to help. If there were tears he needed to cry, then he should cry them.

'I have to care for Rosalie. I have a department to run.'

'Yes, you do. Neither of those job descriptions includes not allowing yourself to grieve.'

'I can't...' He shrugged. 'I can't make sense of that thought.'

'Why not?' She leaned forward, laying her finger on his cheek. 'Look me in the eye, John, and tell me why not.'

That seemed too much of a challenge. His fingers curled around hers, pushing her hand away. But even though he wouldn't look at her, he was still talking and that was something.

'My sister Cara left home when she was eighteen. Fell in with the wrong crowd, and there was quite a bit of drinking and drug-taking. Mum and Dad knew they couldn't compel her to come home but they let her know that they loved her and that they were there for her. No questions asked. Eventually she did come back. Six years ago.'

'She was pregnant?' It didn't take a mathematician...

'Yep. She'd stopped with the drinking and drug-taking as soon as she found out, but she didn't know how she was going to make that resolution stick. Mum got her into a rehab group and that helped a lot. I took a job in a local hospital because I wanted to be there for her too. I used to take her down to the coast and she'd practice screaming at the sea.'

A tear rolled down his cheek. John went to brush it away, and Reba caught his hand. 'Don't deny yourself these memories, just because they're hard. Did screaming at the sea help?'

John shrugged. 'I have no idea, I never tried it. Maybe. Something did because Cara turned her life around, she stayed clean and when Rosalie was born she was a healthy baby. Mum and Dad helped with a deposit on a flat, and we all babysat regularly to give Cara a break. When Rosalie was two, Cara asked me if she could nominate me as Rosalie's adoptive parent, in her will.'

'Was your sister ill?'

'Yes, she was. No one knew it at the time, but she had congestive heart disease, as a result of drug use. I asked her if everything was okay, and Cara said that she was just tying up loose ends and as a single parent she needed to make sure that Rosalie was provided for. The guy she was living with when she became pregnant threw her out as soon as he found out, and said he wanted nothing more to do with her or the baby. Rosalie's birth certificate doesn't name him, and so what she put in her will was legally binding.'

'And you said yes to it?'

'Of course. I'd been a very involved uncle and I loved Rosalie. It was my privilege to be chosen, then and now. I thought I knew all about bringing up a child, but of course I didn't really learn that until I adopted her. But learning's been my privilege as well.'

He fell silent. There was more. All of Reba's instincts told her that there was more.

'I'm so sorry, John. Your sister's loss must have been devastating for you and your parents, and for Rosalie. The way you all seem to support each other…'

'Mum and Dad have been amazing. They were heartbroken when we lost Cara, and no one ever really gets over the loss of a child. But they adore Rosalie.'

'Have you ever talked with them? About how you feel? I've never been in that situation but it

might be a comfort to them to know that someone else is grieving too.'

He shook his head. 'I have to cope.'

That was the heart of it. No one could cope
with something like this without talking about
it, but John was trying and it was eating him
up inside.

'It's a lot. Looking after Rosalie and running
a department—'

Now he looked at her. And there was fury in
his eyes. 'I can cope, Reba. I *have* to.'

She stared at him in shocked silence. Maybe
he understood that there was more he had to say,
because John's expression softened suddenly.

'I'm sorry. I didn't mean to snap.'

'It's okay. Snap all you like.'

'Okay. I didn't *want* to snap then. I was with
someone when Cara died. Elaine had seemed
as happy as I was to be involved with Rosalie
while Cara was alive, and she knew all about
my promise to her. I guess that, like me, she
never thought it would happen because when
Cara died she told me that I couldn't possibly
adopt Rosalie. I'd just got the job as head of department and it was too much. Elaine said that
Rosalie would be better off with my parents or
another adoptive family.'

'Was that her decision to make?'

John shrugged. 'I didn't think so. The plan

was always that we should do as we do now, I'd adopt Rosalie but my parents wanted to be there to help out. It would have affected Elaine, of course, but only because it affected me. I always planned to take full responsibility for Rosalie.'

Reba couldn't get into another person's head. But it didn't sound as if Rosalie's care was really the issue here. She shouldn't say so, bad-mouthing an ex wasn't a good look.

But John was ahead of her. 'I talked about giving up the new job, or going part-time even, but Elaine wouldn't have any of it. She said that if we were going to get married then she wanted to be able to give up work herself and have children.'

'Wait…you were going to get married?'

'Apparently so.' John twisted his mouth. 'That was news to me, although I suppose we might have done, if things had been different. But Elaine had decided what was going to happen next without asking me, and she gave me an ultimatum. It was Rosalie or her. When I told her that I couldn't give Rosalie up, and that I'd make it work somehow, she told me that I'd never cope and she left.'

Everything fell into place. John's assertion that he had nothing to give. Shutting out everything else in his determination to not just cope, but be seen to cope. It was eating him up.

'And Cathy came to your rescue, and helped you become a father.'

'Yeah. My mother was hurting so badly and Cathy knew that and stepped in. She taught me how to make Rosalie happy and I think that in her way Rosalie's helping my mother learn how to be happy again.'

'But *you're* not happy. And you're not really coping either.' Reba wondered whether he would accept that truth from her.

'I don't have anything to give you, Reba. If you had an ounce of sense, you'd run.'

Oh, no. He wasn't going to get away with that.

'Look here, John. This is a devastatingly sad situation, and I don't blame you for feeling as you do. I don't know what I would have done, if I were in your shoes. You can shut me out if you want, but don't you dare tell me to run.'

Something stirred in his eyes. The same response he always gave when Reba resorted to passion. She held out her hand to him.

'You take it or you don't, John. Make your own decision, but be under no illusions that it *is* your decision, because I'm here for you.'

He stared at her. John knew what this meant, and she was asking no small thing of him.

Then suddenly, as if he had to do this before he thought better of it, he reached out to take her hand. 'I don't know what to do, Reba. Will you help me?'

'I don't really know what to do either. But I will help you and we'll muddle through together.' Reba flung herself into his arms, feeling his warmth as he held her close. She needed that warmth, because even though she'd just climbed a mountain to get through to him, there was another, much steeper path to negotiate.

'Have you taken any time off since Cara died?'

She felt him shrug. 'A few days. Mostly things I needed to do with Rosalie's adoption. Mum and Dad took her away for two weeks at Easter.'

'Would you be able to take the day off tomorrow?'

He thought for a moment. 'Probably. What for?'

'Joanne told me that everyone in the department who was close to Cathy was offered grief counselling. I'm assuming you didn't take that offer up.'

'No, I didn't.'

'Then I'd like you to think about making that appointment. Tomorrow if you can.'

She felt his chest heave in a sigh. 'I guess... I don't need a day off to make the appointment, though.'

'No, but maybe you do need to stop for a moment and acknowledge your pain. Take a long walk, or whatever else it is you do to let off steam. Think about it, make the appointment. That's going to be hard if you're really serious about making it work, and not intent on going along and telling the counsellor that everything's all right and that you're coping.'

'Because that would be dishonest, wouldn't it?'

'Yes, it would.'

'Thought so. Would you like to come to bed now? We've only got a couple of hours before it's time to get back up again.'

'So you can forget all about this?'

John chuckled quietly. 'No, that would be dishonest as well. So I can hold you, and just summon up the courage to take you up on your suggestion.'

They'd stayed in bed, dozing in each other's arms, until the very last moment. John had called his line manager, who had reminded him that it was her suggestion that he take a few days off. Reba had seen him smile as he told her that she'd been right all along, and as soon as he ended the call she'd kissed him and raced for the door so that she wouldn't be late for work.

John had called mid-morning, saying that Ro-

salie wanted to come to the music evening, so
Reba had suggested that she bring her home
afterwards. Everything seemed to be slotting
together nicely, to give John a little time alone.
All she needed to know now was whether he'd
made use of that time.

She clung to Rosalie's hand as they walked to
the front door, only letting go when John opened
the door, and Rosalie flew into his open arms.

'I missed you so much!' John looked tired,
but he was smiling. He straightened up, taking
Rosalie with him. 'Did you enjoy your holiday?'

'It was a mini-break, Dad,' Rosalie corrected
him. 'Gramps said that it wasn't a proper holiday but that it felt like one.'

John smiled at Reba over Rosalie's shoulder.
'Okay then. Well, let's invite Reba in then, shall
we? And you can tell me all about your mini-
break.'

So much for finding out how John's day had
gone. Reba had hoped they might get some
time together to talk, but she'd have to wait.
She stepped inside, shutting the door behind
her, and John set Rosalie back onto her feet.
The little girl raced after him, capering around
his legs as he walked through to the kitchen.

A sandwich, along with a small tub of fruit
and jelly seemed to divert Rosalie's attention,
and she decided that she wanted to eat in the

conservatory, as she and her grandparents had done at the hotel. John fetched her a drink, and then he returned to the kitchen.

'So?'

He smiled. 'I had a good mini-break too. I drove out of London and took a long walk. I did think about shouting at a tree, but decided not to. Instead I found somewhere to sit, and made a list of the things that I definitely didn't want to talk about with the counsellor, since they were probably the things that I needed to talk about.'

'Okay. I would have shouted.'

'Yeah, I know. Then I called the hospital's bereavement counsellor. We actually had quite a long chat, which I probably couldn't have done if I'd been at work. I've got an appointment with her on Monday afternoon.'

'Wow. That's quick.'

'She had a cancellation, and she says that she thinks there's a lot to work through.' John turned the corners of his mouth down.

'Well...how do you feel about that?' Reba was trying hard not to put words into his mouth.

'Honestly? Not so good. One thing that today's shown me is that there *is* a lot to work through and... I have a suspicion that's not going to be easy.'

'Probably not. Are you going to stick with it?'

He leaned forward, stealing a kiss from her

lips. 'Yeah. I've decided now, and I'll stick with it.'

However hard it was. However much he had to break down and in spite of how much that was going to hurt. John had made a decision and his relaxed air was because he knew he wouldn't go back on it.

'I've got something for you. For Rosalie, actually. I went home and got my glockenspiel at lunchtime so she could have a try with it.'

'You took a whole hour for lunch?'

Yeah. Reba hadn't felt too good about that, the pile of things she had to do was growing larger by the minute. But this was more important. She held up her car keys.

'Will you carry it in for me? You can't miss it, it's the large black carry case in the boot. Rosalie's bag's in there as well, your mother gave it to me when she brought her along for the music evening.'

He grinned at her, taking the keys from her hand. John returned with Rosalie's pink backpack slung over his shoulder, labouring under the weight of the heavy carry case.

'Are you sure about this? It's heavy enough to be the real deal, not a child's toy.'

'I'm sure. She'll hear the difference, and I've brought a pair of rubber mallets for her so that she can't do any damage.'

'You're fully aware of the destructive capacity of a five-year-old?'

'The whole point of it is that it's a great way to introduce kids to music.' And it mattered that Rosalie had a well-tuned instrument, even if John couldn't hear the difference.

'Okay, if you say so. I'll make sure to keep an eye on her though. Where shall I put it?'

'It has a stand, so in front of the sofa will be just fine for the time being.' Reba moved the coffee table out of the way, and John put the glockenspiel down. She shushed him away and he retreated with Rosalie's bag, sorting through it and throwing clothes into the washing machine.

Reba unclipped the protective case, and extended the stand to what she reckoned would be about the right height for Rosalie. She put one pair of mallets on the coffee table and sat down on the sofa with the other pair in her hand.

John turned suddenly when she started to play. The Shostakovich waltz sounded eerily beautiful when played on the glockenspiel, even if Hans would have labelled the rendition sloppy in places. But John didn't hear that, he just heard the magic.

'That's exquisite.'

'I'm a little out of practice.' Reba skipped back, getting the phrasing right this time. Then she started again, using a little more force with the mallets so that the sound would reach out and find Rosalie.

John was standing quietly, leaning against the counter on the far side of the kitchen. Reba didn't turn when she heard a noise in the doorway, and kept playing. Then she felt Rosalie's hand on her knee.

'You like that?'

Rosalie nodded.

'Okay. Those are yours…' Reba indicated the second pair of mallets, and started to play again. Rosalie ducked quickly around the end of the glockenspiel to fetch the mallets, climbing up onto the sofa and leaning against Reba's arm so she could see what she was doing.

'That's no good, how are you going to reach from there?' Reba curled one arm around Rosalie and the little girl scrambled across her leg so she could stand in front of her.

'Look at how I strike the bars…' she played a few notes '…do you want to try it?'

CHAPTER ELEVEN

REBA WAS AMAZING. Okay, so he was biased, John would admit that. But the way she'd drawn Rosalie in, making her want to play and then helping her to hold the mallets correctly and strike a few notes was pure magic to watch. They'd played a couple of simple tunes together and then Reba had reached into her bag, producing a dog-eared book of tunes, with sticky notes on the ones that she thought Rosalie could manage.

'Here. You can help if Rosalie wants to do some more tomorrow.'

'Tomorrow?' Rosalie tugged at his arm. 'We can do it tomorrow, Dad?'

What was he supposed to do in the face of Rosalie's excitement but swallow his doubts about whether he was up to the task of helping with something he knew precisely nothing about?

'Yes, sweetheart. Reba's going to lend us her

glockenspiel for a few days, so we can play to-morrow if you like.' John was about to remind Rosalie to say thank you, when the little girl turned and flung her arms around Reba's waist. Reba's smile was almost as excited as Rosalie's when she hugged her back.

He sent Rosalie upstairs to clean her teeth, reminding her that the sooner she got into bed the sooner tomorrow would come. Reba picked up her coat and bag, and he walked with her to the front door.

'Thank you.' He bent to brush his lips against hers, and couldn't resist a slightly deeper kiss.

'It's my pleasure.' She wrapped her arms around him in a tight hug. 'Are we all right, John?'

'Better than all right, I'd say. You're sure you don't want to come to lunch on Sunday?'

'I thought I'd pop into the hospital, and catch some of the parents who can't come during the week. But give me a call if you want some company.'

'You get on with what you have to do. It looks as if Rosalie and I will be busy too, we've both got something to learn.' John was beginning to wonder whether Reba hadn't lent the instrument for his benefit as well as Rosalie's. He was looking forward to spending some time helping her.

'I've written down the ABC notation for most

of the tunes in the book. And there's a chart at the back that tells you which bar to hit for each note.'

'Thanks. I was wondering how I was going to work that out. I might give it a read-through tonight. I'll see you on Tuesday.'

Reba reached forward, squeezing his hand. The gesture somehow meant more than any of the words that could have passed between them, and he could let her go now. He watched as she made her way to her car, and then closed the front door.

John was tired. He'd woken at two in the morning for the last three nights, mired in the hollow sensation of loss that he couldn't admit to during the day. He'd come to the conclusion that maybe he should just go with the flow, and gone to bed an hour earlier, getting up when he woke and trying to walk off the feeling that Cara had been taken from his family too soon, by pacing the length of the sitting room, back and forth in an endless repetition of grief.

But the days had been fun. He'd decided to leave the mallets for the glockenspiel where Reba had put them, and let Rosalie pick them up whenever she wanted to, which turned out to be eight o'clock on Saturday morning. John had applied his concentration to which of the bars on the glockenspiel was associated with each note, and then it had become suddenly clear, and he and Rosalie had managed to play a tune together. They'd practised until Rosalie was happy that she'd hit all of the right notes and then John sent a sound file to Reba. Five minutes later he received a call from her, demanding to speak to Rosalie so that she could tell her how beautifully she'd played. Then, late that evening, another sound file appeared in his inbox, which turned out to be a piano accompaniment to Rosalie's tune, which she could play along with.

He sat in his office at eight in the morning on Tuesday, waiting for her. Reba flung open the door without knocking and flipped the switch on his desk that lit the *engaged* light outside.

'Good weekend?' John enquired mildly.

'Yes, actually.'

Reba plumped herself down in a chair. Her hair was done up in a mysterious arrangement which made it look as if it might fall free at any time. John wondered if she might be persuaded to replicate that when they were next truly alone, so that he could find the one pin that released it. He cleared his throat, trying to forget the fantasy of those shiny dark strands caressing her naked shoulders.

'I got quite a bit done on Sunday and I'm feeling pleased with everyone's progress.'

'You were here all day, then?' John felt a little guilty about having been home with Rosalie, making the most of the weekend sunshine.

Reba shrugged. 'Most of it.'

That probably meant from first thing in the morning until the evening. But Reba always looked more relaxed when she was happy with the way things were going with her work, and since he was beginning to understand the healing properties of music for himself he wasn't going to argue.

'So what do I owe the pleasure of this visit to?'

She smiled suddenly. That naked connection, which was overwhelming in their night-time embraces, was only slightly less so when just her gaze met his.

'I was wondering... Do you suppose we should tell anyone? About us...'

'Who were you thinking of telling?' John looked at her, mystified.

'I don't know. I've never had a...thing...with anyone I've worked with before. Do you think HR should know?'

John leant back in his seat, laughing. 'I very much doubt it. You could tell them if it makes you feel any better.' The idea that Reba thought that their relationship was significant enough to notify someone was surprisingly gratifying.

'I don't really *want* to tell them. You're a manager, don't you know what the correct procedure is?'

John applied his rational mind to the situation, remembering what he was supposed to say to anyone from the department who asked about this. 'Well…unless there's a close friendship, a family relationship or a romantic involvement between two people whose work roles are such that one is supervising the other…'

Reba rolled her eyes. 'You mean if I'm sleeping with my boss.'

'Yes. And since I'm not your boss and we each have a different line of senior management, the hospital policy is that it's none of their business. Unless we work closely together and allow personal issues to intrude into our work.' He grinned. 'So no arguing or kissing in the office.'

Reba grinned back. 'Well, strictly speaking that was before…'

'Yeah, well, I don't think they'll be looking for a blow-by-blow account and none of this is going to be a problem. The hospital's not looking to intrude on our personal lives, it's just a matter of making sure that our personal lives don't intrude on the people we work with. I'll mention it in passing to my boss and you can do the same with yours.'

'Yes, okay. That'll put everything straight.'

Reba leaned forward, flipping the switch on his desk to extinguish the *engaged* light on the door.

She was a stickler for doing things right. It was all part of her ambition, Reba wouldn't allow anything to mar what John imagined was a perfect work record. He imagined that she'd be behaving with scrupulous propriety from now on, and that only made thoughts of their nights together more sweet.

'Anything else?'

'As a matter of fact, yes. I'd like to talk to you about Meera.'

The little girl who had been admitted to hospital for surgery on a compound fracture to her leg, and who had been having increasingly frequent asthma attacks. John was concerned about Meera as well.

'Yep. I was going to mention this to you. Before the injury to her leg her asthma was infrequent and under control, but we've had to put her on daily preventer medicine since she's been here.'

'She's under a lot of stress. Her mother said that her injury was a result of having been bullied in the playground and that she was pushed off a climbing frame.'

'Yes, that's right. I gather you've spoken to her counsellor.'

Reba nodded. 'She's happy for me to try and

use music to make Meera feel more calm, and we're going to be working together on that. I'll make sure that I have a session with Meera every day I'm here, and on Sunday I gave her a file with some of the favourite songs that we'd played together when I first saw her. I've got this programme that creates little blobs in time to the music—it's a bit like a sound-sensitive lava lamp and she likes that.'

John chuckled. 'Right. Sounds interesting, I'll have to take a look at it. Meera can use it when you're not here?'

'Yes, she has a tablet that her parents brought in for her. The thing is, though, that I was discussing with her parents how techniques involving relaxation and breathing control can't replace the medicines that she takes for her asthma. They may help with her confidence and make her quality of life better, but if she has an asthma attack then she must use her inhaler. I stress that with all my asthma patients but maybe I didn't need to in this case…'

John nodded. 'I know what you're about to say. Her nurse told me yesterday that there have been a couple of occasions where her mother's called her over saying that Meera won't use her inhaler. It turned out that she wasn't having an asthma attack at all, she was just upset about something and she needed a cuddle.'

'Yes, her mother's very fearful. This isn't a case of an over-protective parent, she's been traumatised too, and she needs support. She was obviously very upset when she told me how Meera was injured, she said that the bullying came completely out of the blue and that the other girls involved were Meera's friends.'

'All right.' John wondered how Reba was going to like this idea. 'I think we need a very joined-up approach to this one. It may be best if you could be there when I visit Meera on my daily rounds, and if I come to a few of the sessions you have with her. Make it clear that we're addressing different aspects of her treatment in ways that are complementary. I know a few people from a local asthma group, so I might have a word and see if they can give Meera's mother some support.'

Reba shot him a suspicious look. 'It wouldn't need to be you, John.'

'No, it could be any one of the doctors on the unit. But I happen to be Meera's doctor, and I'm also taking an interest in how we handle this, because how the different aspects of our work fit together is part of my remit as departmental head.'

'But…we said that we weren't going to bring our relationship into the workplace.'

John sighed. 'I'm not aware that we are. Let's get down to the basics, shall we—is this the best solution for Meera?'

'Yes, I think so.'

'And…don't spare my feelings, here. Do you think that you'll be able to keep your obvious adoration for me under control if we're in the same room together?'

Reba dismissed the idea with a wave of her hand, clearly not in any mood to spare his feelings. 'I don't adore you at all at the moment. Will that do?'

'It'll do. I'm hiding my feeling of mortification very successfully, don't you think?'

That made her smile. Reba was new here, and she seemed to care a great deal about the assessments that other people made of her, always holding herself to a higher standard than she needed to. John guessed that her father's influence featured in that somewhere.

'All right. You're telling me that I can trust you, aren't you?'

If she could bring herself to do so, he'd like that very much. 'I know that your career's important to you. Mine's important to me, and whatever happens between us, stays between us. I'd never do anything to embarrass you or damage your reputation.'

'Thank you. Yours is safe with me, too.' She shot him an impish smile. 'At least during work hours.'

Reba had to admit that she *had* been worried. She knew in her heart that she could trust John, but growing up in a hothouse where the pursuit of excellence had been everything, she'd learned to be wary of anything that might blemish that excellence.

But she'd already learned a lot from John. He might be flawed and struggling, but he was one of the bravest people she'd ever met. When he'd reached out to her and asked for her help, she'd had to bite back her own tears because the gesture had touched her so deeply.

And today there was more to learn. He'd understood her fears and put them to rest with a liberal application of common sense. And when he ushered Reba and Meera's mother into the small private room where Meera was being cared for, the little girl smiled.

It was one thing to make a child smile when their favourite music was a tool of your trade. When you were the bringer of potentially uncomfortable procedures, needles and horrid-tasting medicine, it was quite another.

'How are you doing today, Meera?' He was quiet and undemonstrative, but John's whole demeanour was one of kindness and understanding. Kids had a habit of knowing who was on their side, and Meera was no exception to that rule.

'Okay.'

John nodded sagely. 'I'd like to listen to your chest and take a look at your leg. Just to make sure there's nothing you're not telling me…'

Meera nodded, and John started to examine her. Her leg was *'coming along nicely'*, her heartbeat *'very strong'* and her breathing *'good'*. With each new pronouncement Meera visibly cheered up.

'I hear that Reba's given you some music to listen to.' He sat down on the plastic chair next to her bed, waiting while Meera reached for her tablet to show him. They both chuckled over the way the shapes on the screen moved in time to the music, and John seemed to have all the time in the world when he explained to Meera that the physiotherapist would be coming to see her, to help her get moving again.

'I'm going to have a chat with your mum now, and tell her how well you're doing.' John gave the little girl a parting smile of encouragement. 'Do you have any questions for me?'

Meera shook her head.

'Okay then. I'll be seeing you again this afternoon, so if you think of anything you want to ask me, you can save it up until then.'

'How is she *really*?' Meera's mother asked the question as soon as John closed the door behind them.

'Meera's leg seems to be progressing nicely, she's stable and her chest seems clear. We're monitoring her very regularly, and as you know she's being given medicine which we hope will prevent the asthma attacks.'

'But you won't release her yet, will you? I don't think I can cope with that...' Meera's mother was beginning to look a little tearful again.

'No, we won't be letting her go until we're sure she's stable. And we're doing all we can to achieve that medically and in terms of coping strategies. I'll be liaising closely with Reba and with Meera's counsellor and physiotherapist, so this is very much a joint effort.'

'Thank you, Doctor.'

'And how are you doing?'

Meera's mother brushed the question off with a shrug. 'I'm fine. I just want her to be better.'

John nodded. 'You're only ever as happy as your unhappiest child, eh?'

'Yes.'

'I want you to know that we're here for you, as well as Meera. If you have any questions you can always ask the ward manager to get hold of me. And maybe it would help to talk to a few other parents whose children have asthma?'

Meera's mother shrugged. 'Maybe. I don't know...'

John produced a business card from his pocket and gave it to her. 'This lady runs a group of mums who got together to support each other. You can call her any time, and she's willing to come along to the hospital and meet you. Sometimes it's good to talk with someone whose been in the same situation as you.'

Meera's mother nodded. Despite John's gentle, reassuring manner she looked unconvinced, but at least she put the card into her pocket.

'She's not going to call, is she?' Reba murmured the words as they walked out of the ward together.

'No. Not this time.' He shot her a pained look. 'I can understand that. I just hope she doesn't wait as long as I did...'

CHAPTER TWELVE

ALTHOUGH MEERA WAS everyone's first concern, no one was going to give up on her mother either. Sitting in the corner of the therapy room, John watched as Reba started to work, talking to them both and playing songs that they chose. It seemed light and easy, but beneath it all there was purpose. To find music that Meera and her mother could listen to together, and which might help Meera to breathe and relax.

Reba didn't push, but she was gently guiding the little girl towards finding a way to express her feelings. She invited her to select something from the range of colourful musical instruments that were laid out on a low table, and before long both Meera and her mother were adding their own sounds to the tunes that Reba played.

'That's all we have time for today. I'll see you again on Friday, but in the meantime I'll play some of the songs you've chosen and email the sound files to Dr Thornton.' Reba had been rolling a ball of paper in her hand and suddenly she turned, lobbing it in John's direction. 'Can you put them onto Meera's tablet for her?'

'I'll ask the ward manager, she's pretty good with that kind of thing.' He caught the missile, throwing it back. The sudden lightness in Reba's movements as she reached to catch it made Meera laugh.

'And don't you forget what we've been talking about.' She threw the paper ball gently towards Meera, who batted it towards her mother.

It was a nice way to end a session. Reba's characteristic sense of fun made even Meera's mother smile and hug her daughter, looking suddenly like a different woman. As Reba bent to unlock the brakes on Meera's wheelchair she started to sing, the sound of her voice trailing joy as they walked back to the ward.

May I walk you to your car?

A seven-word text that made Reba thrill with excitement. She texted John, telling him that she had a few things to finish off for the day and she'd meet him in his office in half an hour.

He was sitting behind his desk, grinning. 'So how did your line manager take your revelations?'

Reba had delivered a carefully worded announcement of their new relationship, along with an assurance that it would be kept strictly separate from their work. 'He smiled politely and told me it wasn't an issue. Yours...?'

'She had a bit to say about it.' John chuckled as Reba's eyebrows shot up in panic. 'I got the whole story about how she'd met her husband at work twenty years ago, and how it's good to be with someone who understands the demands of the job.'

So no one considered this was a big deal. Apart from Reba, of course. And John. They both considered it a very big deal.

No one seemed to notice that they were walking in roughly the same direction, at more or less the same time, from John's office on the third floor. But when the distinctive sound of the pager app sounded on John's phone she still jumped guiltily.

'What is it?'

His face darkened. 'Meera.'

The words of annoyance about being pulled back to work just as they were leaving died on her lips. Reba followed John to the ward, where the quiet activity was about as close to panic as things ever got.

Meera's mother was crying as a nurse led her from the room, gently but very firmly. When they entered, the ward manager was with Meera, supporting her in a sitting position as the little girl gasped for breath.

'Inhaler?' John dropped his bag and jacket on the floor in the corner.

'Yes, two doses. It's not making any difference.'

'Do we know why this happened?'

'Apparently she got an email. Her mother was saying it was from someone at her school. Girls…' The ward manager nodded towards Meera's tablet, which was lying on the floor.

John's face darkened. For all the safety that the hospital provided, it hadn't shielded Meera from this. 'Take it away. Reba, over there…' He nodded towards the other side of the bed.

For all his apparent calm, it was clear from his quiet instructions that John was worried. The ward manager picked up the tablet and hurried away to get the drugs that John was now asking for, while Reba took her place at Meera's bedside. The medication was familiar to her and John must consider this a life-threatening situation.

And yet she could do nothing. A tiny part of the helpless anguish that Meera's mother must be feeling gripped at her heart. She sat down, taking hold of Meera's hand, determined that no one was going to have to lead her from the room. If she could bring one ounce of comfort to the little girl, she was staying.

Another doctor arrived, working together with John to administer drugs and oxygen. Meera's lips had taken on a bluish colour, and she was still labouring for breath. When the ward manager arrived, quietly putting a tray down which carried the instruments needed for intubation, a new realisation of the seriousness of this hit Reba hard in the chest. Intubating an asthmatic was a measure of last resort, used only when everything else had failed.

John didn't look round. They hadn't got to that point yet, and Reba didn't dare think about it. She raised Meera's hand to her lips, kissing her fingers, willing her to breathe and listening to John's calm, steady voice as he spoke to Meera, encouraging her.

Fight, darling girl. Breathe... Those words weren't for her to speak, but they sounded over and over again in Reba's head. Meera's small body was beginning to tire in the battle for survival, and her frightened eyes began to close.

'Meera.' John's voice had a slight edge of urgency, as if he were trying to wake her from her sleep. 'Meera...'

The other doctor turned to the tray that contained the instruments for intubation. John shook his head suddenly. 'Give her a minute.'

Just one? One minute before it got to the point where John considered that the drugs weren't working and that another intervention was needed to save her life. One minute before Meera would be intubated and taken down to the ICU, with all the trauma and uncertainty that brought with it, and Reba could do nothing to help stop this.

John was monitoring Meera carefully, ready to make his decision. And suddenly Reba heard her own voice, a little quavery and hoarse, following the notes of one of Meera's favourite songs. John's gaze met hers for a fraction of a second, and she saw him nod her on.

She sucked in a breath, and continued to sing. Surely the minute had passed by now, and John was still tending to Meera, glancing up at the screen which displayed her vital signs every few seconds. She put all of her hope into the song, wondering if Meera even heard it.

'She's responding.'

Maybe the drugs, or the oxygen. Maybe Meera *had* heard the song and kept fighting. Reba didn't care. She continued singing while John and the other doctor cautiously began to consolidate the work they'd already done.

By the time she'd moved on to the third song, John was keeping a watchful eye on Meera while the ward manager made her more comfortable, re-taping the hastily inserted cannula in her arm, humming along with the tune as she did so. A nurse appeared, taking the intubation tray away with her, before leading Meera's mother back into the room. She'd clearly been comforted and told to stay quiet, and Reba jumped from her seat and motioned for her to take her place at Meera's bedside.

'Does she hear us?' Meera's mother asked. An unanswerable question, but John nodded.

'I think she does.'

Meera's mother took a shaky breath and choked on the song that she started to try to sing. Reba put her arm around her and sang with her, seeing John and the ward manager exchanging brief smiles. Meera's eyes fluttered open at the sound of her mother's voice, and now it was Reba's turn to fight back the tears.

Meera's father had arrived, obviously straight from work as he was wearing a suit. John had judged Meera's condition stable enough to leave her with a nurse watching over her, while the worried parents sat by her bedside. He retreated to his office, and after sitting outside the ward for a while, watching the quiet comings and goings of the evening shift, she went to find him.

He laid his phone back down on the desk in front of him, clearly finished with the calls he'd been making. Reba sat down in the chair opposite him, leaving the door open, and he smiled.

'Good choice of song.' His smile broadened as Reba shot him a querying look. 'You don't even know what you were singing, do you? That's the song from Rosalie's favourite film where the prince, who's disguised as a shepherd, is trapped in a cave, and the princess is outside moving the rocks. I've heard it at least two hundred times...'

'Ah, yes. And she sings to him to let him know she's there. No, that didn't really register with me at the time. I just knew it was one of Meera's favourites.'

'Rosalie's too.' John pressed his lips together, a faraway look in his eyes.

Of course he wanted to hug Rosalie right now. Reba could have done with a hug from the little girl as well and she barely knew her.

'Can you call her?'

'I called my mother. She knows this feeling, and she gave me a blow-by-blow account of the football match that my father and Rosalie were having in the garden. Apparently it's looking as if it'll be down to penalties.'

'Why don't you go round there? I'm sure Rosalie could use you on her team.'

'No. She's all right and she can do without me traipsing in for no reason and interrupting her evening.' He flashed Reba a smile. 'And I could do with hugging you too.'

Those quiet moments, when John had waited just a little longer for the medicines to take effect, had brought them closer. If all that Reba had been able to do was to sing, at least she'd done something.

'I wish I could have done more for her.'

'Who knows what any of us did? Maybe it was the drugs and oxygen that pulled Meera through, and maybe she heard the song and knew that she had to fight. Medicine isn't always a science, there's something unknowable there too.'

'I know my limits—'

'Own it, Reba.' The quick exchange might at one time have turned into an argument. Now it was simply encouragement.

'I wouldn't have even thought to do it if you hadn't told me the story about when you met Cathy.' This wasn't all hers to own, it was Cathy's as well. John acknowledged the thought with a smile.

'I notice you haven't asked me about my first counselling session yesterday.' The mention of Cathy's name seemed to prompt John's observation.

'You got my text, didn't you?' Reba had texted him to wish him well and John had texted back after the session to let her know that he hadn't chickened out of it. That was all she'd really needed to know.

'Yes, and it was extremely tactful. I appreciate you not expecting me to say how it went at this stage. I prepared a whole list of things I reckoned I ought to say, and came out having half said a load of completely different things.'

'Sounds promising.' Reba reckoned her comment was vague enough to be encouraging without having any specific expectations.

'I suppose so. You might be in the process of fixing me. I'm not sure yet.'

'I don't need to fix you. You need to fix yourself…' Reba broke off, turning as she heard a noise at the door. Had something happened with Meera…?

A middle-aged woman in jeans and a bright red jacket was standing in the doorway, and John greeted her, beckoning her in.

'Lila. Thanks so much for coming.'

'Much as I adore your company, I didn't come for you, John.' Lila walked into the office, sitting down in the other visitors' chair and flashing Reba a smile.

'This is Reba, our new music therapist. Reba, this is Lila, she runs the support group for parents of asthmatic kids that I was telling you about.'

'Ah, you've taken over from Cathy.' Lila smiled fondly when she mentioned her name. 'She was a good friend of ours, she came to speak with us a couple of times about how music therapy could help people with asthma…'

John leaned back in his seat, rolling his eyes. 'Which is a very thinly veiled hint—'

'Of course it is, John.' Lila interrupted him. 'We didn't grow the group without quite a number of thinly veiled hints, which I hasten to add come with no expectations.'

'Reba's only here two days a week—'

It was Reba's turn to interrupt. 'Thanks, I'd love to come along and chat to your group. Let's make a date.'

'Wonderful. I can promise you as much cake as you can eat. John has my number and we'll fit in with whatever's convenient for you.' Lila beamed at her, and Reba smiled back. She was starting to like Lila.

'Well, if that's all settled…' John paused, waiting for another interruption, and Lila obliged.

'Yes, of course. I gather you have a mum who was distressed when her daughter had an asthma attack this evening.' She turned to Reba. 'I know just how she feels, it happens to us all at one time or another.'

'I gave her your card earlier today, but she

didn't say that she'd call you.' John finally managed to get a whole sentence out.

'I know that feeling too. Not easy to walk into a room full of people you don't know. I'll be very discreet, just introduce myself and give her my address, then leave. I'm only five minutes' walk away from the hospital, Reba, and my husband's a doctor here so we get people popping in all the time. Which is a thinly veiled hint to feel free to do the same. Henry makes a mean cup of Lapsang Souchong.'

'Thanks, I will.'

'So if you'll call the ward manager and tell her I'm on my way, and to let me in, John…' Lila got to her feet.

'Sure. Thanks Lila.' John picked up his phone and made the call, while Lila wished Reba a good evening and hurried away.

'So, what are the odds?' Reba smiled at him as he put the phone back onto his desk.

'Of Meera's mum just taking Lila's address and letting her go? Not great, I imagine. But Lila *is* very discreet and she won't intrude where she's not wanted.'

'She seems nice. Is the Henry who makes a mean cup of Lapsang Souchong the same Henry who's head of Orthopaedics here?'

'Yep. He and Lila are good people.' John pinched the bridge of his nose, stress and fatigue

showing in the gesture. 'I'd like to stay for a little while longer, just to make sure that everything's okay with Meera and her parents. Would
you like to give tonight a miss? Or I could come
over to you when I'm finished here?'

Reba wanted to stay too, but she hadn't been
sure how to ask. 'That fits in with me perfectly.
I'll be here for at least another hour. I need to
tidy my cupboard.'

'Ah. Urgent cupboard-tidying.' He grinned
suddenly. 'If you're sure…'

'I'm sure. We can pick up a takeaway on the
way home from the Chinese restaurant around
the corner from me. Eat it at the kitchen table,
and then you can sing me to sleep.'

'A takeaway sounds great. You don't want
me to sing you to sleep though. The bad things
that Rosalie says about my singing really aren't
exaggerations…'

CHAPTER THIRTEEN

OUTWARDLY, EVERYTHING SEEMED to be falling into place. For the last three weeks, John had spent all of his free nights with Reba, and missed her during the weekends, which was okay because there were always texts, and calls that left him under no illusions that even though she was working she was also missing him. Rosalie had navigated the bumpy one-year anniversary of her mother's death, and seemed to be blossoming again. John was feeling much more equal to the demands of his job, and although his twice-a-week counselling sessions still perplexed the life out of him he still felt that he took something away from them every time.

Inside, the numbness that he'd felt for the last year seemed to be wearing off. That was good and bad. Anger, frustration and grief were difficult bedfellows, and John still woke in the night burning with helpless rage. But Reba... Who wouldn't want to feel every exquisite moment spent with her? To be able to react to her music, and match her passion.

He hadn't got around to telling his counsellor about his relationship with Reba yet, because he didn't consider it to be a problem. Which meant the question of whether and when he might ask if Reba would like to spend some time with him and Rosalie at the weekends had gone un-answered as well. But Rosalie had clearly been cooking up some ideas of her own.

'No! Don't record me, Dad!' Rosalie carefully put the mallets down on the glockenspiel and then flounced off into the sitting room. John switched his phone off and followed her.

'Okay. I'm sorry, I should have asked you first. Would it be okay to make a recording later to send to Reba?'

'No!' Rosalie sat down on the sofa, crossing her arms. 'I want Reba to come *here* to listen. I'll make pizza for her.'

'All right. So you'd like me to ask her over for pizza and you'll play the glockenspiel.'

'No, Dad.' Rosalie gave him a look that plainly said he was being a little slow. Some-times she was so much like Cara, and John al-most recoiled from the mixture of pleasure and pain. 'I can ask her for myself.'

John wondered how Reba might take that. Perhaps a quick phone call first to check… But

Rosalie was already on her feet and on her way into the kitchen.

'Hold it right there, Rosie.' John managed to cut her off before she got to his phone.

'I can do it, Dad.'

Yeah, that was exactly what he was afraid of. He thumbed the shortcut to the text conversations between him and Reba, and started to type.

'I've just got a text from someone at the hospital and I need to answer that first.' John supposed that technically Reba was someone at the hospital, even if their text exchanges rarely had anything to do with work.

'All right.' Rosalie was used to the odd phone call from work over the weekends, and retreated back into the sitting room. John waited for a reply to his text, wondering whether he should close the door and call Reba instead, to explain a bit more fully.

It's okay. Let Rosalie call me.

The text was accompanied by three hearts, which quietened his mind a little. All the same he texted back.

Sure?

His phone rang. Reba plunged straight into the conversation, much as she usually did.

'Are you okay with this, John?'

'Yes. Absolutely.'

'She's within earshot, isn't she? On a scale of one to ten, ten being that you'd really like me to come and one—'

'Ten.' John didn't need to know what one was. He walked forward, closing the kitchen door. 'I'd love it if you came round for pizza with us, but only if you're ready. I know you've been here before, but this feels as if we're making things official.'

'I'm not even remotely ready.' Reba chuckled. 'But it's something you'd like to do and so would I, so let's just do it. We're both adults, and if Rosalie comes up with any surprises then we can deal with them.'

That was one of the many things he liked about Reba. She was unafraid, without the caution that loss had ingrained in him.

'All right. Don't say you didn't ask for this...' He walked into the sitting room, handing the phone to Rosalie.

'Will you come for pizza tomorrow? I'll play the glock...en...spiel for you.'

Reba seemed to be talking for a little longer than it would normally take to say yes. Rosalie was listening carefully.

'Can we go to the seaside as well?'

Another pause, and then Rosalie turned her head up towards him.

'Reba says I have to ask you, Dad. Can we go to the seaside?'

'That sounds nice. Did Reba say she'd come tomorrow?'

Rosalie nodded. John waited while she had a conversation about the glockenspiel, telling Reba all about how they practised at weekends, and then Rosalie ended the call and dropped the phone back into his hand, climbing up into his lap and giving him a hug. Clearly he'd done something right.

'What time is Reba coming?'

'Tomorrow.'

'Okay…' His phone buzzed and he opened the text from Reba, which contained the answer to his question. 'She'll be here at nine o'clock, so we'd better be ready to leave by then…'

Reba was less sure about this than she'd made out. She'd spent time with John and Rosalie before, but as their relationship had started to deepen there was an unspoken rule that it should be kept away from Rosalie, just as it was kept away from work. Something that was between themselves and didn't have to answer to the everyday.

And then there was the work that she'd intended to do this Sunday. She'd looked regretfully at the musical scores that she'd been planning to convert into child-friendly display boards so that the children under her care could play a short piece together. It didn't really matter if that waited a week, but somehow it felt that her purpose in life was slowly being diluted. As if she was moving away from everything that Hans had taught her.

But the excitement of arriving on a sunny Sunday morning for a trip to the seaside outweighed all of that. John had prepared a cool bag full of food, and they'd decided to head for Brighton and then along the coast to a beach where John had promised they could go fossicking for treasure.

The famous chalk cliffs undulated gently for miles to the east of Brighton. John seemed to know where he was going, and Rosalie was already excitedly clutching a small plastic bucket on her lap. He parked the car at the top of the cliffs and they looked down on a sand and pebble beach, strewn with white boulders that had been smoothed by the sea. Ahead of them, steps zigzagged their way down the cliff face.

'What do you think? Not quite the place for getting sand between your toes and drinking cocktails.' John grinned down at her. He was keeping a tight hold on Rosalie's hand, but she was jumping and hallooing with excitement.

'It's wonderful. Much more interesting than sand and cocktails.'

'I think so too.' He turned back to the car. 'Let's get you ready for an expedition, Rosie.'

Rosalie sat on the tailgate of the vehicle while John got her into a windcheater, waterproof trousers and a pair of non-slip neoprene-soled shoes. A magnifying glass was hung around her neck inside her jacket, and a notebook and pen tucked into her pocket. Finally a little sou'wester with flowers on it that matched her jacket was tied under her chin.

'You look so cute, Rosalie!' Reba squatted down on her heels in front of the little girl.

'Cute?' John feigned an expression of mild outrage, pulling on a windcheater and shouldering a small backpack. 'What are we, Rosie?'

'Explorers!' Rosalie raised her arms, shouting at the top of her voice.

John nodded, handing Reba her waterproof jacket and a large plastic bucket with a fitted lid. 'Are we ready to go?'

They walked down the steps and onto the beach, turning to look at the white cliff towering above them. Rosalie ran to the nearest outcrop of rocks, her head down, looking for treasure already.

'You're right, she does look unbearably cute, doesn't she?' John grinned down at Reba. 'As do you…'

They spent hours, sorting through shells and stones on the beach, bending over rock pools to catch sight of small crabs scuttling to and fro and digging holes in the sand. John's back-pack had all kinds of useful items in it, a book to identify the wildlife they saw around them, a torch and an underwater viewer that allowed Rosalie and Reba to take turns in looking at the inhabitants of the rock pools without disturbing them.

It was hungry work. They found a smooth flat rock to sit on, and John went back to the car to fetch their lunch. Reba helped Rosalie untie the bow beneath her chin, putting the sou'wester into her pocket before it blew away down the beach.

'I came here before. With Mummy and Uncle John.' Rosalie was sorting through her bucket now, picking out stones and shells that caught her eye. 'It was a long, long time ago. Uncle John's my dad now.'

Reba looked up at John, who'd just reached the top of the cliff steps. Maybe she should put this conversation off until he returned, but Rosalie was looking at her, expecting an answer.

'Did you have fun?'

Rosalie nodded. 'We were explorers then too.'

'And are you having fun today?' Reba hardly dared ask. Rosalie's mother was no longer here, and perhaps the little girl didn't want her to be replaced by anyone else, even if it was just for a seaside outing.

'Yes. I'm bigger now, so I can climb up higher. Are you having fun?'

Reba smiled. 'Yes, I am. Thank you for letting me come with you.'

'That's all right. You can come again if you want to.' Rosalie picked a piece of sea glass from her bucket. 'I like this one. What is it?'

'It's called sea glass—it's ordinary glass that's been in the sea for a while, so that it's smooth and frosted over. It takes a long time for that to happen, but it's really pretty, isn't it?'

Rosalie nodded, looking up at the beach behind them. 'Dad! Look! I found a piece of sea glass.'

John was striding towards them, grinning. 'That's a great find, Rosie. You know that sea glass is magic, don't you?'

Rosalie frowned at him. 'It's just glass that's been in the sea for a very, very long time. Maybe a whole year, I don't really know.'

'Ah. Well, I stand corrected, then. Put it in your pocket and I'll zip it up so that you don't lose it, eh?' John put the bag down, pulling out a packet of wet wipes. 'Then we can clean our hands and have something to eat.'

John had prepared a stack of sandwiches, and they'd eaten nearly all of them. He and Reba sat together, sipping coffee from the vacuum flask, while Rosalie took the box of juice that John had given her and wandered towards a nearby collection of stones, looking for any that caught her eye.

'Rosalie told me that she remembers coming here before. With you and your sister Cara.'

'She remembers that?' John's eyebrows shot up in guilty surprise. 'We used to go out exploring a lot together. Cara loved the sea and we'd usually end up on a beach. We only came here once, though.'

Gently. Go gently.

Reba had a hundred questions, but they had to be asked one by one.

'She called you Uncle John.'

'Yeah, she does that sometimes. Particularly if she's talking about something that happened before Cara died. I suppose it's her way of distinguishing between then and now.'

'Rosalie said you're her dad now.'

John thought for a moment. 'That's a nice way of putting it. That's what I want to be to her.'

He was staring at Rosalie now. He'd been

watchful all day, never letting her out of his sight and keeping her within his reach if they were climbing. But now he appeared to be trying to see inside the little girl's head, just by the force of his gaze. That wasn't going to work.

'She seemed to want to talk about it. She told me she'd been here before right out of the blue.'

A pulse began to beat at the side of John's brow. Maybe she'd gone too far.

'I find it hard to know what to say to her sometimes. I don't want to push her. My parents are a lot better at this than I am. Rosalie's always coming up with things that my mum or dad have told her about Cara. I guess they've had a bit more practice at being parents, I'm still learning.'

'I wonder if they'd say that they're still learning too?'

'Probably. What do *you* think?'

Reba puffed out a breath. 'I know even less about being a parent than you do. But you're a doctor, and you deal with kids every day. How would you approach a child in your care?'

'I'd…make space for them to talk. Then leave the decision about whether they want to talk up to them.'

'Yes. That's what I'd do too. Only I'd probably put a percussion instrument into their hand at the same time, in case they wanted to make a noise.'

John thought for a moment and then emptied the dregs of his coffee onto the stones around their makeshift picnic area, dropping the cup back into the cool bag. 'Do you mind...?'

'Of course not. Go.'

She watched as John walked over to Rosalie, squatting down on his heels beside her. The little girl showed him her newest finds, and John patiently looked at each of them in turn. Then she saw him indicate the cliffs with his finger, asking a question. Rosalie's hand strayed to his knee as she moved a little closer to her dad.

John picked her up so that they could talk face to face as he strolled slowly down towards the sea. They seemed to be in their own world, Rosalie safe in his arms, her small hands clinging to John's shoulders. It was a picture so intimate that it seemed wrong to even look at them, and Reba started to gather the remains of the lunch things together, putting them back into the bag.

When she zipped the cool bag closed again, looking up, Rosalie was walking next to John, back up the beach towards her. John was smiling, and when Reba waved to them both, Rosalie waved back.

'We've decided we'd like to shout at the sea.'

John's grin broadened when Reba raised her eyebrows.

'Dad says that you like to shout…'

'I didn't quite say *that*, Rosie…'

'So you have to come and help us.' Rosalie ignored John's protest.

'I'd love to come and help you. Your dad's right, I'm really good at shouting. If you shout at the sea you have to do it as loudly as you can.' Reba wondered if the shouting was really just for her and Rosalie, and John would just open his mouth, letting nothing out.

They walked back down to the shore together, and Rosalie chose their spot.

'Let's go then, Rosalie…' Reba grinned down at her. 'Three… Two… One!'

Reba shouted as loudly as she could and Rosalie jumped up and down, waving her arms and hallooing wildly. And then suddenly from behind them came a loud, deep bellow, shot through with strands of despair and pain. But as John's roar reached the open sea, the only thing that Reba could hear was hope…

They'd shouted, and John had skimmed stones into the sea, much to Rosalie's delight. Reba and Rosalie had sung in the car on the way home, and John had tapped his finger on the steering wheel. The plan for smiley-faced pizzas had been abandoned in favour of a huge takeaway pizza, and they sat on the sofa in the kitchen eating slices with Rosalie's haul of shells and stones scattered on the table in front of them.

When the little girl began to yawn, John waited while she kissed Reba goodnight and then lifted her up, taking her upstairs to bed, while Reba sorted through the pile of oddly shaped stones that Rosalie had declared were dinosaur bones, arranging them in a row on the table. John came back down the stairs ten minutes later.

'Out like a light. She barely managed to clean her teeth...' He sat down next to Reba on the sofa. 'Thanks for coming today. I had a really good time.'

'Me too. Thanks for asking me.' Reba leaned forward, picking up the stone that she'd set to one side. 'I think Rosalie's managed to find a *real* fossil.'

'Really?' John took the stone from her hand, looking at it. There was the clear imprint of a tiny shell, half obscured by a thin slice of stone. 'I think you're right. I wonder if I could prise off that piece at the side to see all of it.'

'Looks as if it might come off. You'd have to be careful.'

'Yeah. On second thoughts, I wouldn't want to damage it. I'll make sure that Rosalie keeps that one, it's a real find.' He leaned back on the sofa, his arm resting on the cushions behind her. Reba shifted a little closer, leaning against his shoulder.

Just a few moments. Then she'd go home…

Reba drifted into wakefulness. She was lying on top of John, his arm curled around her shoulder. And there was light coming from somewhere… Had they slept through the alarm…?

She sat up suddenly, hearing him grunt softly as her elbow dug into his chest. The light was still on in the kitchen and she had her clothes on. She cursed under her breath as he began to move, opening his eyes in the same panicked process that she'd just been through.

'What time is it?' John shook his head, as if trying to gather his wits.

Reba focused on her watch. 'Two o'clock.'

'Okay. It's no problem. I'll get Rosie up and put her in the car, and take you home.'

'No, that's not going to work. You take me home and come back here. So in the morning I'm stuck without a car, and I need my car because I'm doing some home visits.'

'Then…' John thought for a moment. 'You drive your car, I'll follow you and see you home. That'll be better, won't it.'

'No, it won't. Think about it for one minute

and tell me how you get to be less vulnerable than I am when you have Rosalie sleeping in the back seat of your car.'

'Stay here, then. In the spare room.'

His brow was creased, and a pulse beat at the side of his temple. John didn't want that and Reba didn't need it. She was awake now, and the thought of spending the night here seemed suddenly far too complicated.

'I'll be perfectly all right. You can watch me to my car if you feel you must. I live alone, and it's been known for me to go out after dark and drive home in the early hours of the morning before now.'

'But…you don't need to. I know we'd decided not to tell Rosalie about us just yet, but she's got to know sooner or later.'

But his first reaction was all that Reba saw. He'd been afraid, and Reba had to admit that she had too. Not of telling Rosalie, because she was sure that could be managed. He was afraid of the same things that she was. That telling Rosalie meant a commitment to a relationship, when they both knew that they were only in the early stages of fixing the things that stood between them.

'Look, John. You're making a mountain out of a molehill. I'm going to do what I planned on doing all along, and go home. Just kiss me goodbye and let me go, will you.'

'Okay. I guess…' He drew her into his arms, hugging her. 'I don't mean to insinuate that you don't know how to look after yourself.'

'I know.' She snuggled against him, wondering if this wasn't exactly where she wanted to be. Which was why she really had to go home…

He switched the light over the front door on, watching as she walked down the front path. Reba got into her car, locking the doors and flashing the headlights in a signal to him that he could go inside now. Fifteen minutes later, when she stepped inside her own front door, she called him and John answered on the first ring.

'All safe and sound. I'll see you on Tuesday.'

'Thanks, I appreciate you calling. Sorry if I came on too strong.'

'It's okay. We had such a nice day today, and I didn't want to end by rushing into anything before we'd decided it was the right thing for all of us. I came on too strong too.'

'First argument?'

'First of many, let's hope.' Reba made a stab at a joke, and heard John laugh quietly.

'I'll make it up to you when I see you. Goodnight, sweetheart.'

Reba ended the call, puffing out a breath. John had been her perfect man from the very start. A committed doctor, who understood why she'd made the choices she had for her own career. Perceptive, kind... She could spend all day writing a list of things she loved about him. All night with a list of things they got up to when the sun went down.

He'd been broken and he'd struggled against the immediate chemistry between them as hard as Reba had. But he was strong enough to mend, to try and put the past behind him and make a place in his heart where they could be together.

Reba had been trying too. She'd been driven to succeed by a childhood that had been moulded around the pursuit of excellence, and an adulthood that had been marked a disappointment by her own father. She was beginning to come to terms with that now.

But what if she couldn't change? What if she broke John's valiant heart? Or hurt Rosalie, who'd already been through so much? Reba had tried to balance her work with this new relationship and it had been a constant battle, one that she'd only won because John had commitments of his own. How would she manage if they took the next step and she found she wasn't as strong as John, and couldn't leave her past behind her?

She was too tired for this, too confused to think straight. Reba stumbled up the stairs, catching the scent of the sea in her clothes as she pulled them off. Maybe tomorrow would take care of itself, because suddenly Reba wasn't sure what to do.

John was coming slowly to the realisation that something was the matter. Their telephone conversation on Monday evening hadn't lasted as long as usual, but Reba obviously had a project of some sort on hand and he dismissed the thought. He was just being paranoid. On Tuesday she'd made her apologies and said she couldn't make their date that evening. That was okay, she had a life and it didn't always fit around his. Whatever she was doing was clearly consuming her attention because she apologised again on Wednesday, saying she couldn't make Thursday evening either.

It wasn't so much that he missed her. Or that he clearly wasn't going to be able to see her this week. But Reba *never* apologised for working, and she wasn't usually as vague about what was going on with her. He missed the Reba who might sometimes speak first and think later, but who always told him what was on her mind.

The days dragged by, punctuated by the regular evening calls, that seemed to have lost some of the ebullient sparkle that Reba brought to them. On Friday he abused his position as head of department, and asked Joanne if she had a copy of Reba's appointments diary for the day, since he wanted to know when she was free for lunch. She tutted and showed him how to look it up on the department's intranet, and then John had all the information he needed.

CHAPTER FOURTEEN

Car park. Now.

THERE WAS ONLY one reason why the head of the children's unit would want to meet with the music therapist in the hospital car park. Reba supposed that she deserved to be called to account for her actions.

She'd been working with the kind of focus that was unusual even for her. Guilt and uncertainty had spurred her on, and she'd been busy for every second of the time that she usually spent with John, telling herself that she wasn't really avoiding him but just giving herself some time to think things through.

And now it was all catching up with her. The worst of it was that she was no less confused than she'd been at the start of the week.

She could have texted back and told him no. But John deserved an explanation, even if she didn't have one to give. She opened the doors that led out of the therapy room and into the garden, cutting across the grass to the car park. She could see John standing by his car, watching as she approached.

'You have an hour for lunch?'

'Yes. But John, I'm not going to spend it arguing with you here.' It would have been better to meet in his office. At least that wasn't a shortcut from one side of the hospital campus to the other, and overlooked by rows of windows on one side of the main building.

'No. We're not going to argue here.' He opened the passenger door of his car, walking round to get into the driver's seat. Fair enough. This had to happen.

He was quiet, but seemed almost relaxed as he drove out of the hospital gates. The fifteen-minute drive to his house was made in silence, as Reba tried to get her muddled thoughts in order.

No such luck. He parked on the hard standing outside his house, and Reba stayed resolutely in her seat. 'Why did we have to come all the way here?'

'Frank exchange of views.' He seemed really committed to the idea that this wasn't an argument. 'We can't do it at work, and so we'll have to do it here.'

'But John…' He'd got out of the car now and

had unlocked the front door. Reba hurried after him. 'Listen, we've talked about all of this. You said that you didn't want it to be all about when you're free and that you respect that there'll be times when I'm not.'

'And that's still the case. But you're making excuses, and you've *never* made excuses for anything. It's one of the things I love about you.'

Love. That word. It had been intruding into her own thoughts for the last week, taunting her that it was way beyond her capability to love anyone as much as she loved her work. That was why she'd deliberately avoided John, because he was the answer to that question.

And John had gone and said it now. The man who kept his feelings under wraps, who pretended that everything was going smoothly while he raged inside… He'd said the word *love*. That was how far they'd come together, and Reba felt a sudden, unwelcome warmth for him in her heart.

'This is confusing me, John.' It was the one honest thing she'd said to him all week and he knew it. His lip curled in an expression of triumph.

'Great. Really, that's great. It's a place to start. Reba, I know that you're ambitious. I know that you care about your work and that you have something to prove. That doesn't mean that you have to shut me out—'

'Yes, it *does*.' A second piece of the truth flew from her lips. 'You're right, I do have something to prove, and I'm not particularly proud of that. You're the one person that makes me forget all about it.'

He stared at her. 'You mean…? Actually, Reba, I have no idea what you mean. You're telling me that our relationship is too good for its own good?'

'I don't want to hurt you, John. Our relationship meant change for both of us, and I'm fully aware that you've been a great deal better at that than I have. What if I don't have it in me to change?'

He flung up his hands in an expression of frustration. 'When was the last time you decided you wanted to do something, and then bottled out because you thought you couldn't?'

Reba thought for a moment, her mind suddenly a blank.

'I'm waiting…'

'Stop it, John. You're a normal person. You're kind and brave and you know how the world works. I didn't grow up like that. I was taught that the only thing that matters is achievement.'

John puffed out a breath, turning away from

her. The light in his eyes was hidden now, and suddenly Reba felt cold.

'Did you honestly think…' He turned suddenly, his eyes blazing. 'Did you think that I wouldn't be there for you, Reba? After you've been so present, so clear-sighted with me.'

'I'm afraid that I'll let you down and I won't be there for you. When we fell asleep at your house I saw you were worried that Rosalie might find out about us, but when you thought about it you were willing to take that step. When I thought about it, all that I could think of was that I wasn't ready and I was afraid.'

'But do you want to be?'

'Yes. That's never changed. It's not just the amazing sex…'

He smiled suddenly. 'Mind-blowing… Is that what it's really supposed to be like?'

'You're asking *me*?' Even when they argued, the honesty and the love was still there between them.

He held out his hand to her. 'Take it, Reba. I don't know what's going to happen next, and there are a lot of ways that we could both be hurt. I'm able to take that risk now and I want you to trust me and take it with me.'

Suddenly she was in his arms. They were both trembling, and this felt…so good. As if John really could protect her from an unknown future that might involve a little failure but might involve the biggest success of all.

A thud sounded from upstairs and they both jumped. John stepped away from her, quietly taking her arm and moving her towards the front door.

Did you leave a window open? Reba mouthed the words up at him and John shook his head.

Then footsteps. He opened the front door, clearly about to push her outside, and Reba wriggled against his grasp. If he thought he was going to face an intruder alone, then John had another think coming. Then a voice.

'John... Darling?'

John froze. 'Mum?'

Babs appeared at the top of the staircase, looking flustered. 'John, I'm so sorry. Did I give you a fright? The school called to say that Rosalie had left her workbook at home, so I thought I'd collect it and then drop it in for her. I was just looking for it when I heard you come in. You were obviously engaged in...something important...and I should have called out, but... I sat down on the bed and blocked my ears...'

John swallowed hard. To his credit, he made no attempt to run.

'It's okay, Mum. I should have realised it might be you.'

'I imagine you had other things on your

mind...' Babs was walking down the stairs, clutching Rosalie's book. 'Hello Reba. So nice to see you again.'

Perhaps Babs hadn't heard the part about the mind-blowing sex. 'Lovely to see you too, Dr Thornton.'

'You can't be having amazing sex with my son and call me Dr Thornton. Babs, please.' Reba saw John close his eyes, probably trying to convince himself that this wasn't happening.

Reba stepped forward, her knees shaking. 'I'm really sorry, Babs. We've managed to get ourselves into an awkward situation, and I didn't mean to embarrass you.'

Babs seemed to be weighing the question up. 'I think it's for the best. You two clearly need some time together to sort things out between you and so I think that Rosalie should stay with us tonight. You can come and collect her tomorrow afternoon some time, John.'

'That's not necessary, Mum. You're supposed to be going out for the evening.' John was struggling to hide his embarrassment and not succeeding very well.

'That's all right, darling. Irene's already cried off and Maggie and Tim are on holiday in Paris, so we were talking about cancelling this week. And this is important. You don't take enough time for yourself.'

He could say no. John could insist that they didn't need to take Babs up on her offer and that would be an end to it. But she and John *did* have things to work out. One sentence had changed everything—*Did you think that I wouldn't be there for you?*

'Thanks, Mum. I really appreciate it.' He turned to Reba, his face full of warmth. 'What do you reckon, Reba?'

'I reckon that Friday evening and Saturday morning might be just what we need.' She saw a flash of knowing humour in Babs' eyes. 'To talk…'

'Right then.' Babs straightened. 'Well, I'll be off now. Don't talk too much, will you. In my experience, actions are far more reflective of your real feelings, and they speak a little louder sometimes.'

John ignored the comment. 'Thanks, Mum. I'll see you on Saturday.'

'Yes, and both of you come for a late lunch if you're free.' Babs hugged John and kissed him, then took hold of Reba's hand, kissing her cheek. And then she was gone, leaving both John and Reba staring after her.

John cleared his throat awkwardly. 'How much do you think she heard?'

Reba doubted that Babs really had had her

hands pressed to her ears, but she reckoned that John needed that element of doubt.

'I don't think we should dwell on that.'

'No. Probably not.' He thought for a moment. 'Was my mother *really* telling us that she thought we should iron out our differences in bed?'

The words *amazing* and *mind-blowing* might have contributed to Babs' stance on that one.

'Yes. I think she was, but we probably shouldn't dwell on that too much either.'

'There's really only one thing I want to say to you, Reba. I know that we can't fix each other, we have to do that for ourselves. But you've already given me the space that I need, and it would be my privilege to give you the space that you need. If we can be honest and accept each other on those terms, I'd love to keep working and playing, arguing and loving with you.'

'I would too, John. I was frightened, but… I don't feel that way now.' Reba laid her hand on his arm, standing on her toes to plant a kiss on his cheek.

He returned the kiss, brushing his lips softly against hers. 'Until tonight, then.'

'Yes. Until tonight.'

They had to leave now if they were going to be back at work in time. As John turned the corner at the end of his road, looking out for the traffic, Reba saw Babs' car parked on the busier main road. She was about to wind down the window and wave when she realised that Babs had her phone pressed to her ear and was deep in conversation.

Probably cancelling her night out tonight. John didn't need to know about that, but Reba would remember to thank Babs with a bunch of flowers the next time she saw her.

John was a happy man. All of the women in his life appeared to be conspiring against him, but that did nothing to take the edge off his contentment.

Rosalie had informed him that Grandma was teaching her to knit, and that she needed to go and look at lengths of wood with Gramps because he was building a new shed. This was all better done on Sunday mornings, and since they needed to get an early start it would be better if she spent Saturday night at Grandma's house. The words obviously came straight from his mother's mouth, with a few embellishments from Rosalie, and John gave his approval to the plan.

His mother and Reba seemed to be engaging in flower wars, each giving the other thoughtful little arrangements where points were scored for originality rather than size. They'd taken to laughing together in the kitchen, and John had decided that he was better off not knowing what the jokes were about.

And Reba. John had made it clear to her that he supported her ambition, and she'd clearly taken that on board. Their time together might be limited, because of his schedule as well as hers, but it was full of golden moments that reached out into his dealings during the rest of the week.

Last night they'd sprawled naked on her bed, and Reba had carefully set out carved chessmen on a board between them. If he'd wondered whether this might be an exercise in seeing how long they could concentrate before they were distracted, then he was wrong. Reba played to win, and since the unforced error which had sacrificed two of his men had been the result of John's preoccupation with the way her hair fell across her breasts, he'd demanded a rematch. This time he'd managed to capture her queen, but then Reba had won again with a beautifully executed pincer move that he hadn't seen coming. When she'd offered him the chance to make it the best of five he'd declined, carefully laying the board aside and lovingly executing a few moves of his own.

But he reckoned that today would be the biggest challenge for Reba. A whole Sunday afternoon spent with nothing to do.

The fete was an established feature in the life of the hospital, and much the same as it had been when John and Cara went with their parents as children. There was a large bookstall, a games tent for the kids, refreshments and a band, along with a few friendly sporting activities for those who wanted to take part. It all provided a framework for staff, patients and half the local community to turn up and spend an afternoon in the sun.

Reba had enquired tactfully what the provisions for music would be and when she was told that the brass band that was playing had been an essential part of the afternoon for the last twenty years she'd expressed her delight and backed off. John happened to know that it would have taken her a few phone calls to summon world class musicians, ready to take part in a Sunday afternoon jamming session for charity, but, however tempting that was, Reba didn't like to step on anyone else's toes. The Friends of the Hospital had the refreshments in hand, so it appeared that Reba would be consigned to a deckchair for the afternoon.

But she was nothing if not a team player. Reba donned a filmy feminine dress, perfect for a Sunday afternoon fete, inspected the contents of the bookstall with John's father and cheered Rosalie on in the games tent. This might not be the most sophisticated event in the world, but everyone made an effort and it was always a lot of fun.

'Can't *you* play?' They were sitting on the grass, watching the races, and Rosalie lolled to one side, leaning against Reba's arm.

'No, sweetie. There's a brass band.'

Rosalie frowned, clearly not impressed. 'They play the wrong notes.'

'Only one or two. That doesn't matter if you're playing with your heart, does it?'

Rosalie shrugged, jumping to her feet as the staff three-legged race was announced, which she'd already decided was her favourite race. 'Dad… Dad!'

'I'm just going to watch.' John leaned back on his elbows.

'But you could do it with Gramps…' Rosalie's face took on an imploring look and John shook his head. 'Or Reba.'

'No, Rosie, Reba doesn't want to get her dress dirty.' John remembered Reba telling him that contact sports weren't her thing when he'd suggested rounders to her.

'Reba…?' Rosalie turned her pleading look onto her. 'You'll only get dirty if you fall over, and my dad will hold you up.'

Reba grinned suddenly. 'Okay, why not? What do you reckon, John?'

'You're sure?'

'What's the worst that could happen?'

They took their places at the starting line, and Reba took off her shoes and knotted the hem of her dress so that it wouldn't get in the way. There was some delay as everyone tied the fabric bindings around their ankles, and John rolled up his trouser leg, taking off his own shoes so that he wouldn't be in danger of crushing Reba's toes.

'We can get into a rhythm. I'll call the steps, since my legs are shorter than yours.'

'Yeah, okay. Are we going to win this, then?'

Reba looked along the line of competitors. 'Of course we are.'

It looked as if they might for the first half of the course. And then Rosalie started to squeal with excitement from the side of the course and Reba looked round, momentarily losing her concentration. She reached for him as she lost her balance, but her fingers only grazed his arm and John couldn't stop her from falling. It was as much as he could do to stop himself from falling on top of her, and he landed on both hands, one on each side of her.

'Are you okay?' She'd fallen on her side, one arm beneath her body.

'Yes...' Reba grimaced as the other competitors thundered past them. 'We're not going to win now, are we.'

'That doesn't matter. Did you hurt yourself?'

'Couple of bruises, I expect, but I'm all right. No excuse for us to spend too long lying here like this.' She rolled onto her back, laughing, but as she pulled her right arm out from under her she yelped in pain.

John looked down and realised why. Her index and middle fingers were both at a sickening angle, obviously broken or dislocated. And Reba was beginning to cry...

The one thing about being injured at a hospital fete was that there were plenty of people on hand to help. He felt someone untying the fabric around his and Reba's ankles, and when he levered himself away from Reba an ambulance paramedic checked her over quickly and gently sat her up.

'John... John, my fingers.' She was reaching for him, and he caught hold of her left hand.

'Okay. You're okay. It looks worse than it is.'

The paramedic shot him a glance. It might not look worse than it was, but Reba was almost hysterical now, and he knew that she was seeing her music stripped away from her by one fall. Someone appeared with a wheelchair, but she wouldn't let go of him and so he lifted her gently in his arms, carrying her into the hospital.

Reba was trying to keep it all under control. Trying not to look at her fingers as John set her back onto her feet, walking her into the radiology department. Babs arrived with their shoes and, since there was no queue, John rapped briskly on the door to the X-ray room, which was opened by a technician.

'Dr John Thornton. I'll do the paperwork later. I need a lateral and posteroanterior hand view.'

'You can come straight through.'

In a daze, Reba sat down next to the X-ray machine. John was arranging her fingers carefully on the table, and the technician retreated into her cabin.

'I'll be gone for one minute. Just stay still.'

'I can't… I can't feel them, John. They don't even hurt.'

'You're in mild shock right now. They'll start to hurt later.' He tipped her face around. 'Don't look at them, just close your eyes. Trust me.'

Closing her eyes didn't help much, because all she could see were the grotesquely twisted fingers. Her bow hand. How was she going to play the violin now? Reba began to feel sick and opened her eyes, closing them again when she caught sight of her injured fingers. They actually did look worse when she looked at them.

Everything seemed to be going out of focus. She remembered John slipping her shoes onto her feet and replying that his parents were looking after Rosalie when she asked about her. The lift up to his office. People hovering around, and John firmly shepherding everyone away, apart from one man who sat down opposite her.

'I'm Henry. I believe you've met my wife, Lila.'

'Lila. Yes. Who are you?'

'Dr Henry Poste. Head of Orthopaedics.' Henry smiled at her.

'Good. That's good, thank you. Where's John?'

'Right here.' John closed the door behind the last of the people who'd gathered to help, pulling a third chair over to sit next to her. 'Henry's the best.'

'Kind of you to say so.' Henry smiled, leaning towards Reba. 'I am, of course. Now, let's take a look at your hand, and hopefully we'll have the X-rays in a few minutes.'

John held one hand while Henry gently examined the other. There was a short pause while John opened his laptop and logged on to pick up the X-ray files, and Henry looked at them carefully while John stood behind him, looking at the screen.

'Well. Good news, I believe. Your fingers are dislocated, as we can all see, but there are no broken bones.' Henry peered at the screen. 'There's a very tiny chip of bone in your index finger. Right there, John, you see it?'

'Uh...no.' John leaned in, squinting at the screen. 'Ah, yes.'

'It's very small and that's not going to be a problem. The bone will heal naturally, and there are no fractures. We can reduce the dislocations, give you supports for your fingers, which you must wear for a while, and you'll be as right as rain.'

'Thank you.' Reba breathed a sigh of relief. 'They're starting to throb a bit now.'

'Yes, they will. That's all to be expected. Would you like to see the X-rays?'

'No. Thank you.' Looking at her fingers was hard enough, let alone X-rays. But Henry's reassurance had already made her feel a little better. 'I play the violin. And the piano...'

'Well, of course you'll have to take a break from both for a while, but once your fingers have healed you will be able to play the piano. And the violin, naturally.' Henry chortled at his own joke. 'I've been waiting to say that for many years.'

'Too soon, Henry,' John murmured and Reba managed to summon a smile.

'No, it's not too soon. Thank you.'

The process of setting her fingers straight again wasn't as painful as she'd expected. John had fetched a canister of gas and air and sat beside her, holding the mask in case she needed it. But Henry was swift and precise in his movements, and the pain didn't last long. He applied padded splints to both her fingers and suddenly Reba could look at her hand again and examine the bruises that were forming at the base of her fingers without feeling sick. A sling to immobilise the hand made it feel far more comfortable, and John proffered two paracetamol and a glass of water.

'You'll take Reba home, John?' Henry asked.

'Yes, and I'll stay with her to make sure she's all right.'

'Well, then, I won't need to go through the list of dos and don'ts, I'm sure John is perfectly capable of that.' Henry reached out, taking her left hand and giving it a reassuring squeeze. 'It's been a pleasure to meet you, Reba. I only wish it were in better circumstances.'

'Thank you.' Was that the hundredth or two hundredth time she'd thanked him? Reba wasn't sure but she meant every one of them. 'I really appreciate all you've done.'

'I'd better be off to see how Lila's doing. We

have four grandchildren and it usually takes both of us to manage them all…'

Reba had put on a smile when John took her downstairs and out into the sunlight. Babs was sitting with Rosalie under a sunshade at the corner of the grassed area where the fete was still in full swing, and as soon as she caught sight of Reba and John she jumped up, running over to them.

'Are you all right?' Rosalie was leaning against her father's leg, looking at Reba uncertainly, and John put a comforting hand on her shoulder.

'Yes, thank you. I'm fine. No harm done.'

Rosalie craned up, trying to get a glimpse of her hand. 'Your fingers were crooked. I saw them.'

Rosalie must have run forward when she'd fallen. Reba felt herself redden with remorse. 'Well, they're not now. Your dad X-rayed them for me, and Dr Poste straightened them up. Look.'

Reba bent down so that Rosalie could see inside the sling, and wiggled her fingers as much as she could. The sudden throbbing was worth it, because Rosalie nodded in satisfaction.

'My dad will make you better.'

Reba swallowed down the lump in her throat.

No one could make this better. She hadn't injured her hand too badly, but this was a sudden, bitter taste of what it would be like to lose everything she'd worked so hard to achieve. John was a good man, and he'd persuaded her that she could change. The panic and horror she'd felt when she'd thought she might lose her ability to work had brought the truth home to her. She couldn't change, and John deserved better than that.

'I'm going to take Reba home and look after her. Will you help by being a good girl for Grandma and Gramps tonight?'

'Yes, Dad.'

'Okay. Give me a hug…' John swept his daughter off her feet, kissing her, and Rosalie chuckled delightedly. Babs walked over, giving Reba a kiss and telling her to take care, and then John ushered her over to his car. Reba relaxed back into the front seat with a sigh of relief.

'I'm so sorry, Reba.' John didn't start the engine when he climbed into the car.

'Sorry? What for? You've been looking after me so well.'

'I should have stopped you.'

'What do you reckon the odds are of competing in a three-legged race and coming away with two dislocated fingers? And since when do you get to stop me from doing anything?'

'I still wish I'd tried.'

'You did try. You told Rosalie that I wasn't going to take part and then I said I would.' It had been that pleading look that Rosalie gave her. Wanting to do something to make her happy. To make John happy. When she'd looked at her fingers her first thought was to resent him for it, and Reba was thanking her lucky stars that she'd been too dazed to voice the undeserved sentiment.

She leaned across, laying her hand on his arm before he reached to start the car. 'Just take me home, I don't need you to stay. I'll be fine and you should be with Rosalie.'

John shook his head. 'No. You're not kicking me out tonight. This time I *do* get to stop you.'

A part of her wanted to be alone, but another part wanted him to stay. Just one last night sleeping next to him, in the hope that she might be able to persuade herself that she could deserve John.

'Okay. Thanks. I'll do as you say.'

He nodded, starting the car. 'Now I *know* you're not well enough to be left on your own.'

CHAPTER FIFTEEN

JOHN HAD LEFT Reba on Monday morning with strict instructions to call him if she needed anything. This fall, the injury, had shaken her badly. Anyone would be shaken by it, but for Reba it meant more than just the physical ramifications. It had threatened everything she'd worked so hard to be, and all that she was so driven to achieve.

He'd taken Rosalie to see her for an hour on Monday evening, and she'd seemed better. More settled, as if she'd made up her mind that this was just a temporary setback. Which was why it was such a shock when she answered the door to him on Tuesday evening.

She looked pale and drawn, as if she hadn't slept a wink last night. Reba walked into the sitting room and lowered herself into an armchair, unable to even raise a smile.

'What's the matter, Reba?'

'I've been thinking, John, and I have something to say to you.'

'Okay. Fire away.' The beginnings of dread curled around his heart. He knew how to meet Reba's passion, whether it took the form of anger or love. John had never seen her so devoid of any emotion, and she didn't seem to be the woman he knew any more.

'I'm going to leave my job at the hospital, John.'

'But... There's no need for that, is there? Henry said that it's just a matter of keeping your fingers supported for a while, and they'll be fine. Has he been in touch and told you any different?'

'No. When I go back to work I'll be concentrating on my private practice for a while.'

It took a moment for what she was saying to sink in. 'I don't understand. Are you telling me that you're leaving *me*?'

'Yes. I'm sorry, but that's exactly what I'm telling you.'

Something cold settled around his heart. There had been passion right from the start in their relationship, but there was none here. He could hardly even bring himself to ask Reba why she was doing this, but he couldn't leave without knowing.

'Why, Reba?'

'You fixed yourself, John, and I can't. I've never had a relationship that's lasted longer than a few months, and it's because I can't focus on more than one thing at a time. That's the way I was taught to be, and I don't know anything else.'

'And we can't just love each other for what we are?' John could feel the world beginning to close in on him again. The numbness of loss, and the sure knowledge that he would carry that burden and keep going.

'I don't think we can. I've tried to do the work that I need to, so that we can both move on together, but I'm not sure that I know how to. This is my fault and I'm sorry for the pain it's causing, but carrying on is only going to make it hurt even more.'

Pain? He could hardly feel it. Maybe he'd start to feel the throb in time, but right now all he could feel was shock. Reba must know what that was like, she'd experienced much the same on a physical level when she'd fallen.

'I've made sure that the children's unit is covered for a music therapist. The colleague that I work with at my private practice, who filled in for me today, has experience at a number of different hospitals and she's willing to stay for as long as she's needed. She's very talented, and

I've told her that she can call me at any time if she has any questions.'

'That's fine. I met her today and she seems very capable.'

They were down to this. Temporary cover for her job and handover periods. There really was nothing more. They'd had all of the highs and lows, Reba had helped John to fight for himself and then he'd fought to keep her, but every victory just seemed to make her less able to cope with their relationship.

And he'd failed her. He knew that Reba was vulnerable, but he hadn't been able to reach the part of her that constantly drove her on to succeed.

'I should go.'

Reba nodded. 'As you wish, John.'

No, he didn't wish this at all. But there was no point in telling Reba that because her mind was made up. His was too, now. Reba had paid a high price for loving him. Her injury would heal, but she would still be torn between spending time with him and working to appease the voices in her head that only accepted excellence as being good enough.

'I'll have the glockenspiel delivered back to you in the next few days.' One last end to tie up. He knew that Reba's musical instruments were precious.

He got to his feet and Reba sprang to hers. She followed him out into the hallway, seeming to lose her composure for a moment.

'If... Maybe she doesn't... Whatever you think's best. It's up to you...'

A glimpse of Reba's tendency to open her mouth before she'd decided what to say. Suddenly he could feel again, and it hurt so badly he caught his breath.

'I mean...' Reba turned the corners of her mouth down. 'If Rosalie would like to keep the glockenspiel then it's hers. I'd really like her to have it. Tell her to keep playing with her heart.'

John didn't know what to say to that. It was a generous gesture, and it meant that he wouldn't have to explain to Rosalie why she had to lose the instrument that she loved. But he was done with generosity and love now.

'We'll see. I don't know.' He turned, opening the front door, and walked to his car. Nothing hurt any more.

John had taken to leaving his office door open. Every time someone knocked and opened the door a little too quickly he couldn't help remembering how Reba had always flown into his office with an armful of challenges for him. That constant reminder that she was no longer here was a pain that he could do without.

He'd discussed their parting with his counsellor—or rather talked about it while she nodded and asked a few questions. John supposed that was how non-directive counselling worked, but he wished she could come up with a formula to make it hurt a little less. Or maybe hurt a little more. There were times when he got through the day just by cultivating a feeling of numbness.

His mother had asked after Reba and he'd told her they were no longer together.

'I'm sorry to hear that. I like Reba very much.' His mother thought for a moment. 'Would you like us to take Rosalie for a couple of weeks?'

John shook his head. 'To be honest, Rosie's about the only thing keeping me going at the moment. You can't mope around with a five-year-old in the house.'

'Exactly. You know that there were days when I couldn't get out of bed after Cara died, but you always coped. You looked after Rosalie so well.'

'It was different for me.'

'Maybe... But losing Cara was still hard for you. I never quite forgave Elaine for her attitude to it all.'

'I don't think about her all that much now.' Elaine was a pale shadow from the past, obscured by the vibrant colour that Reba had brought.

'I can't say I'm sorry to hear you say that…'
His mother puffed out a sigh. 'Look, John, I
don't want to meddle but I can see you're upset.
I really think you should let your father and me
take Rosalie for a little while. It's about time you
stopped coping.'

Reba had said something of the same. Warmth
and pain rushed into his heart at the thought,
almost bringing tears to his eyes.

'I might take two weeks off work.'

'Do it. You've hardly had any time off in the
last year, you must have plenty of leave saved
up. Aren't you going to lose it if you don't take
it?'

'Maybe. I hadn't really thought about it.'

'John! Am I going to have to nag you about
this?'

The glimmer of something began to flutter
in his heart. He'd been paralysed before he met
Reba, and could do nothing to help himself. But
she'd given him the tools to mend, and he knew
how to do it now. It wouldn't be easy, but things
that were really worth it never were.

John set out at six on a Saturday morning a
week later. And just drove. That night he stayed
in a pub just outside Melton Mowbray, and the
following night in a rather smart hotel in York-
shire that happened to have a vacancy. He was a

traveller, with no fixed abode for the week and no particular place to go.

On the fourth day he found himself in Scotland, and drove north past mountains and lochs. The wild countryside, and the fact that he'd hardly spoken to anyone in the last four days, hadn't provided him with any sudden revelations about the way that life worked, and John still didn't know what he was hoping for.

He found somewhere to stop for lunch, taking his sandwiches down to a deserted waterside and sitting down. It was breathtakingly beautiful here, and as he ate alone he seemed to find her again. Reba's smile in the rippling loch. Her dark hair in the shadows that moved across the sunlit hillside. Her sudden passion as birds rose in perfect synchronicity in response to a sound across the water.

Something brushed against his cheek, cool in the breeze. When he raised his hand to brush it away he felt tears.

'Reba. Reba.'

He murmured her name and then heard it echo back amongst the hillsides as he shouted across the water.

Reba!

Things were not going well. The first annoyance was that it took twice as long to do even simple tasks with two fingers in splints and when you were supposed to keep that hand immobilised as much as possible. Typing and keyboard work was awkward one-handed and, since she was right-handed, writing was impossible. Dressing was time-consuming and she was running out of easy-care clothes that didn't have buttons or need ironing.

Maybe it would have been better if Reba could have worked her feelings out with a few exhaustingly angsty pieces of music, but playing either the violin or the piano was out of the question at the moment. And work was difficult. She could do many of the things that she usually did in her therapy sessions, but wasn't happy with giving her clients any less than a hundred percent. Her colleagues at the private practice had taken over most of her caseload, which left Reba trying to do as much as she could to help but at a loose end for most of the time.

These things would pass and they were just the tip of the iceberg. Everything else would have been bearable if she hadn't missed John so much. She was angry with herself for being the one who'd broken them apart, and she was angry with him… She didn't know why she was angry with John, he'd done nothing wrong. But sometimes being angry was a little less painful than just missing him. There was no going

236 CHILDREN'S DOC TO HEAL HER HEART

back because it was her own way of life that had come between them. And when she woke in the night, crying for him, it seemed that she would still be missing him on the day that she died.

This morning was going to be different. She said that to herself every morning and these days it never was. Reba tumbled out of bed, going through the annoying process of showering one-handed, fixing her hair and getting dressed. Today she would be recording the music of the river.

Saturday morning strollers were walking along the path that ran past the side of her house, and Reba tucked a note into her letterbox, in case the parcel she was expecting arrived this morning. She climbed carefully down the short sloping bank, staying within sight of her front door so that a courier would find her, and sat down in the grass. A startled duck flapped away across the water before she could get the microphone out of her pocket, and she cursed. That might have been a good one...

She sat for an hour in the sun, not getting a great deal done but it was slightly more constructive than moping inside the house. When she heard footsteps behind her, swishing through the long grass, she wondered whether she should record those...

'Reba?'

She froze. Didn't dare look around. Then John sat down beside her.

'What are you doing out here?'

'What sort of question's that?' she bit back at him automatically, already hurt by three weeks of having to do without his smile.

He looked great. His hair was a shade blonder, as if it had seen some sunshine recently, and it suited him. And here by the water his eyes seemed a little less grey and a little more blue.

'It's one of those throwaway opening questions. When you have no idea what to say to someone.'

Reba's heart started to beat faster. His relaxed air suited him a little better than the buttoned-up man she'd first met. She was beginning to feel frumpy, sitting here in an oversized sweatshirt, with rings under her eyes from too little sleep.

But she knew John. If he was here then he had a reason. It wasn't just curiosity or to throw something at her in revenge for all the hurt she'd caused. And, despite herself, despite knowing that there was no hope for their relationship, she wanted to hear what he had to say.

'I'm recording sounds. Maybe matching them up with music at some point, I'm not sure yet. I haven't thought it all through yet.'

He nodded. 'So you're bored.'

'Yeah. What are you doing here?' That was the zillion-dollar question.

'I didn't like the way we left things between us. I wanted to try and make that right.'

Closure, then. Maybe his counsellor had put John up to this, but Reba didn't imagine that it had been all her idea. John was more of a leader than a follower.

'I don't think we can make it right, can we?'

'I wouldn't be here if I believed that. Reba, there's something I want to say to you.'

'Would you like to come inside?' Reba instantly regretted the question. She'd been plumbing new depths of untidiness lately.

'Wherever you're most comfortable.'

'Here's nice.'

He nodded, looking at the gently flowing water in front of him. 'I've been thinking about that night, when you held out your hand and challenged me to reach out. I want to thank you for being there for me when I was in crisis. For telling me the hard truths that I didn't want to hear.'

Reba swallowed down the lump in her throat. 'You made it work, John. It was worth it.'

'I told you once that I wanted you just as you are. That was the truth, but I let you down by telling you that. You cared enough to see the

man that I could be and not the one that I was,
and to challenge me to change.'

'It was obvious…'

He nodded, shooting her a wry smile. 'Then
I'll return the challenge. You have to stop seeing
yourself through your father's eyes and value
the things that make *you* happy.'

It was simpler and a lot more straightforward
to just go on as she always had, putting everything else second to her work. But suddenly,
faced with all that she'd lost, that hurt too much
to even think about.

'So this breakup is going to be the most ci-
vilised ever? We'll be friends who can tell each
other anything.' Reba hit back at him again.
Trying to deny her own pain and the truth in
his words.

'No. I can't be your friend because I'll always
want more. I love you, but I have to learn to live
without you. I don't know how I'm going to do
that yet, but you've given me hope that I might
just work it out.'

'John, just… I appreciate what you're saying but just go. Please, I can't take this.' Reba
felt tears pricking at the corners of her eyes.
She blinked them back and saw his beautiful
eyes fill with tears. John *had* changed and at
this moment all she wanted was to be able to
do the same.

'Just one more thing?'

'One. No more.'

He felt in his pocket and then took her hand, dropping something into it. Keeping his fingers around hers so she couldn't look at what was there.

'I'll always love you and be there if you need me, and…you can throw this away if you want to. Just hold it in your hand and count to ten first, and know that you have a piece of my heart. You'll never be able to give that back because it's freely given, with no expectation of anything in return.'

They were both trembling. 'Go, John. Please.'

He got to his feet and walked away without looking back. Reba opened her hand and saw a piece of blue sea glass that she recognised as one of the treasures that John had shown her, kept from his childhood. Held in place by a tracery of silver wire, it hung from a silver chain.

She raised her hand, ready to throw it into the river.

Count to ten…

It felt as if it was burning a hole in her palm, but before she got to ten she found herself holding the sea glass to her heart, crying bittersweet tears.

'Are you all right, love?' A voice sounded

from the path behind her and Reba turned, wiping her face with the sleeve of her sweatshirt.

'Yes. Thank you, I'm fine.'

And Reba had things to do. She stood up, putting the microphone and recorder back into her pocket, and made for her front door with all the purpose that had been missing from her life since she'd lost John.

The house in Berlin was beautiful, with soaring white-painted spaces and a grand piano which took up a whole section of the huge open-plan ground floor. Reba hugged her mother and father, ignoring Hans' dismay at the supports around her fingers.

'It's fine. It'll heal.'

'I'll make an appointment for you with my doctor in Harley Street.'

'No, you won't, Hans. I had the head of Orthopaedics at my hospital do the reductions and he's the best there is. And free.'

Hans shrugged. 'You should have only the *very* best, Rebekah.'

'That's what *best there is* means. The very best.' It appeared that Reba wasn't going to have to find a way to broach the subject that she'd come here to talk about. She'd been here for five minutes and Hans was already doing it for her.

It was good to see her parents, though. Hans

was creative, funny and a great raconteur and her mother was the anchor of the family with an easy-going warmth that Reba had missed. They went out for dinner at one of the best restaurants in Berlin, strolling through the streets afterwards so that her parents could point out places of interest to her.

Her mother was an early riser, leaving Reba and Hans sunk in their armchairs talking while she took her book with her to bed. Reba had been afraid of this moment, knowing that it was coming, but somehow it didn't seem quite so confronting now that it was here. She laid her hand on the blue sea glass pendant around her neck, to remind herself of all the reasons she had for doing this.

'I've missed you, Reba. We used to be so close.'

'I've missed you too. It's one of the reasons I came.'

Hans regarded her thoughtfully. 'To clear the air?'

'Yes, actually. I didn't know that you were aware that the air needed clearing, though.'

'You think I didn't notice that I haven't seen you for two years.'

'I've been busy. And a little cross.' Rebecca took a sip of her nightcap. 'And I'm wondering why I don't call you Dad.'

'You've always been my equal, Reba, even when you were a little girl.'

'No. That's my point. I wasn't your equal. I was your child.'

Hans narrowed his eyes. 'You think I was a bad father? You may be right.'

'I think you were a great father. You showed me things and places that many people never get to see and you taught me how to make wonderful music. You loved me and I'm grateful to you for all that.'

'But…?'

Reba took a breath. 'Can you help a child who's had brain damage speak again? Or comfort a child in pain, or help them to express themselves? Because I can. That's my calling, my passion. It's not second best and I haven't sold anyone short—neither you or me.'

'And I mustn't say that. Is that what you mean?'

'No, you're at liberty to say whatever you want. But I want to ask something of you.'

'Anything, Reba.' Hans' face became grave. He knew that she was serious about this.

'I want you to support me in the career I've chosen for myself. Because it was a good choice and it makes me happy. I'm asking you to do it against all of your own inclinations and for just one reason. Because you're my father.'

'You never said this before.'

'No, I didn't. Because I'm your child, and your judgement matters to me.' Reba was quivering with anxiety. But Hans seemed perplexed rather than angry.

'Tomorrow I want you to tell me all about it. About the children whose lives you can change and about the music. And I promise I'll listen to you. But in the meantime... Can we play?'

Maybe he'd mellowed. Maybe Reba had grown up a bit. Or maybe stones drawn from the sea really did have magical properties. Reba wasn't sure, but her hand strayed again to the sea glass that hung around her neck, tucked into the neckline of her top.

'I'd really like that. I haven't played since... this.' She held up her fingers, turning the corners of her mouth down.

It was nice to sit on the long piano stool with him. Beethoven for three hands took a little improvisation, but Hans' choice was one of those little jokes that they both understood without explanations. Beethoven had been deaf and yet continued to compose despite it all, so two fingers that were sure to heal weren't such a hill to climb in comparison.

Reba led, and Hans fell into step alongside her. Effortless, if you didn't count the hours of practice that were a way of life for them both. Soaring in the cavernous space, and yet intensely personal. And she missed John so much…

'Dad…' She stopped playing, her shoulders shaking, tears running down her face. Her father's concentration broke suddenly and he put his arm around her shoulders, comforting her.

'What is it, Reba?'

'Dad, I've been a fool. And I think I've really messed up…'

CHAPTER SIXTEEN

SOME THINGS JUST HURT, whichever way you cut them. John had said what he'd wanted to say to Reba, done what he'd wanted to do. He felt a little more at peace with himself, as if he'd repaid some of the enormous debt that he owed her. But that didn't stop the pain or the grief at losing her. There was no getting around going through the hard stuff.

The worst parts of it were when he was alone at home. No longer on the open road, with the feeling of movement to lull him. Without Rosalie, or his parents or any of the people at the hospital whose company seemed to insulate him from what was going on in his heart. When he was alone he had to face it all.

He'd taken to sitting in the conservatory as the sky darkened, the doors into the garden slightly ajar so that he had the company of the noises of the night along with his thoughts. The strains of music drifting in the quiet air seemed a natural progression to loving Reba and for a moment he didn't move, simply enjoying the strains of Clair de Lune that were floating in his mind.

Clair de Lune…? It sounded a little different when Reba played it on the violin but the sadness remained. The longing that seemed to permeate every note. When he got to his feet, flinging open the doors, he saw her.

Dressed in black, as if she were playing to a full concert hall, her face seeming to shine in the moonlight. A piece of blue sea glass suspended around her neck. The supports around two fingers of her right hand meant she was holding the bow a little awkwardly, but the music was still the same. She must have seen him, but she kept playing until he was close enough to reach out and touch her.

'You came.' Maybe she'd been summoned by his thoughts and it occurred to John that she might not be here at all.

Reba smiled up at him. No fantasy could have fabricated Reba's smile, or the effect that it had on him.

'I love you, John. I couldn't stay away.'

Her words gave him the courage to take the violin and the bow from her hands, the first time he'd dared touch either of them. But she didn't reach to retrieve them, back into the safety of her grasp. Reba followed him into the conservatory and he laid the instrument down carefully on the long sideboard.

'Am I too late?' She looked up at him.

'How could you be? Always is a very long time…' The shock of seeing Reba again was beginning to recede now, and John realised that he needed to say the words as much as she seemed to need to hear them. 'I love you, Reba. Now and for ever.'

She reached for him and he curled his arms around her, hearing her own trembling sigh mirror his own.

'I've been doing a lot of thinking. A lot of talking as well. I went to Berlin to see my father and I said some things that he needed to hear a long time ago.'

She could tell him about that later. There was only one more thing that John wanted to hear now. 'Will you stay?'

'Yes. You're my centre, John. The thing that holds everything else together and gives it meaning. I can't promise to always get it right, but I'm here for that as well.'

It was all he needed to know. Everything else would fall into place around that. They could talk later.

'May I kiss you?'

'I think you should. We've already had to wait too long.'

John held her close, kissing her, feeling the accompaniment of passion that always ran through their most tender embraces.

'This is everything, Reba. Your love is all that I want, and everything I need.'

Her lips curved against his. 'This is just the start, John. We have everything to look forward to.'

EPILOGUE

One year later

REBA HAD PLANNED everything down to the last detail. She'd given John a printed spreadsheet detailing where everyone would be, and at what time, and there was one gap. From nine until nine-thirty, after the hairdresser had left and before her bridesmaids arrived, she'd be alone at home.

John slipped his door key into the lock, entering the quiet house. It was different now. When Reba had sold her house they'd stored all of her furniture in the garage and had taken their time in integrating their households. Reba's eclectic exuberance somehow blended perfectly with his fondness for calm, natural surroundings and now their home seemed a great deal more than the sum of its parts.

When he walked upstairs he saw a chair in the hallway, outside their bedroom. Tapping gently on the door, he sat down and heard Reba call his name.

'Not like you to leave a whole half hour un-accounted for.' He grinned, leaning against the door that separated them.

'It isn't, is it. What must I have been thinking?'

She'd been thinking the same as he had. Reba wanted to do things properly and John had stayed with Rosalie at his parents' house last night. But if it was bad luck for him to see his bride on the morning of their wedding, there was nothing to prevent him from hearing her. Just as she did with everything else, Reba had turned the accepted way of doing things into something that was deliciously theirs alone.

'How's my dad doing?'

John chuckled. 'Surprisingly well. I think he took the lecture that you gave him about this being *our* day to heart.' The choice of music for the ceremony had been something of a sticking point between Reba and her father, but Reba had stood firm and Hans had capitulated. He still spoke his mind, but now that Reba had learned to expect him to accept her choices, he did so.

'You'll make sure he's here by eleven, won't you? I don't want him rushing in at the last moment.'

'He was already looking at his watch when I left.'

John heard Reba laugh. 'And you've got your buttonhole from the florist?'

'Yes. Mum cried when she saw her corsage. That was such a nice thing to do.'

Reba had asked John about Cara's favourite flowers, and John had told her that she loved the purple hues of violets and lilacs. So Reba had chosen lilacs for her own bouquet, and matching shades for the buttonholes and corsages. Rosalie loved her pale lilac bridesmaid's dress, and the fresh flowers that she would wear in a headband.

'Babs is okay, though?'

'Yes, she's a lot better than okay. I'm not sure she realised how much she'd love it, when we asked her about the idea.'

'I can't wait, John. I love you so much.' He heard the brush of her fingers against the other side of the door, and raised his own hand to touch it.

'Did you look? You can tell me…'

Reba laughed. For months John had been heading her off when she tried to sneak to the end of the garden and see the inside of the large music room that he'd been building as a wedding present for her.

'No, I didn't look—where's the fun in that? Is it finished?'

'Yes, it's finished. So any time you like we can move your music room from the spare bedroom, and come up with some ideas about what we can do with an extra bedroom.'

'I could buy you a train set...' Reba's voice took on a teasing note.

'Nah. I like the colours you picked for a nursery.'

'Me too...' He heard Reba sigh. 'You're going to have to sneak out before long, if the bridesmaids aren't going to catch you here.'

'Yeah. Just a few moments more.' John pressed his hand against the door, knowing that Reba was doing the same...

It had been worth the wait. Reba appeared at the entrance to the church exactly on time, and Hans accompanied her proudly down the aisle. She looked so beautiful, in a simple white dress with flowers in her hair and a bouquet of exuberant colour.

Rosalie was the star of the show. Her bridesmaid's duties were carefully choreographed to fit in with a four-handed piano piece with Hans, who skilfully made her role shine while his supported it. When Hans nudged her into standing up and giving a bow, the wedding guests turned into an audience and applauded, led by the bride and groom.

'Thank you for making me so happy, John.' Reba danced in his arms in the huge marquee, to the music that was being played by an assortment of the guests. 'I love you always.'

'I love you too, Reba.' He twirled her round, accompanied by an impromptu swell in the melody. 'Always.'

'Sickness and health. Agreements and disagreements.' She kissed him.

'All of it. Especially the disagreements.'

* * * * *

*If you enjoyed this story, check out
these other great reads from
Annie Claydon*

Cinderella in the Surgeon's Castle
Snowbound with Her Off-Limits GP
Stranded with the Island Doctor
From the Night Shift to Forever

All available now!